D0814560

PAY THE LINE!

John Gollehon

A PERIGEE BOOK

Perigee Books
are published by
The Putnam Publishing Group
200 Madison Avenue
New York, NY 10016

First Perigee Edition 1988

Photo credits:
Casino interiors at the Desert Inn,
Kelly-Van de Stadt, Las Vegas.

ISBN 0-399-51459-7

Printed in the United States of America
1   2   3   4   5   6   7   8   9   10

The author wishes to express his appreciation to:

The Desert Inn, Las Vegas, NV and casino manager
Russell Scott
The Claridge Hotel, Atlantic City, NJ, and casino
administrator Paul J. Burst
The MGM Grand, Reno, NV and dice manager,
Richard Brock
The Las Vegas Convention and Visitors Authority
The Las Vegas News Bureau
The Atlantic City Casino Hotel Association
The Reno Convention & Visitors Authority
The South Lake Tahoe Visitors Bureau, and marketing
director Bob Anderson

To my mother, Edna, the only player I know who can expertly split 10's.

To my wife, Kathy, who didn't ask for a divorce while I was writing this book at home...in the bedroom.

To my six-year-old son, Johnny, who drew some interesting "spaceships" on my manuscript.

About the Author:

John Gollehon is president of a leading electronics manufacturing firm in Grand Rapids, Michigan. An accomplished engineer, designer, and instructor, Mr. Gollehon is perfectly suited for designing a new Player Concept, and teaching the new concept to both the beginner and advanced player in a sensible, "engineered" approach to beating the casino.

His insight and vast knowledge of casino games go far beyond the games themselves. In fact, it's the author's contention that most players lose because they are "conditioned" to lose . . . lacking the skills and discipline to formulate a serious game-plan. Surprisingly, Mr. Gollehon has found in his studies that most players honestly anticipate losing!

The author's sole objective is to "recondition" the player in a winning frame of mind. Like any successful athlete, the player must have confidence and determination to win!

Although recognized as an expert player, Mr. Gollehon has no ties to the casino industry. **Pay the Line** has been written by a player, not a casino executive, who stands on the same side of the tables as you do.

CONTENTS

THE FABULOUS "STRIP" IN LAS VEGAS.

INTRODUCTION

Pay the Line is an expression of winning at the dice tables. An appropriate name for my book. I could easily have titled it, "Seven-Out." But that's an expression of losing. The book simply wouldn't sell. Everyone already knows how to lose!

There's a particular purpose to *Pay the Line* that hit me soundly as I watched a popular Nevada casino fill up with players. A casino that offered perhaps the worst playing conditions for blackjack imaginable.

I counted over twenty blackjack tables, all with six decks! Double-downs were severely restricted. The dealer hit soft 17's. Most assuredly, surrender was not offered. Even the dice tables were *only* single-odds.

On this particular evening, the casino was jammed. Players were drawn to this plush casino, obviously not aware that a better game, with far better rules, was just across the street. Single-deck games with full double-down privileges! Around the corner, surrender was offered with four decks. And the crap tables were all double-odds! No one knew, and no one cared.

I watched players splitting face-cards. Afraid to hit stiffs. Indecisive! Like going to war without guns.

There were players at the dice tables making asinine bets,

one after another. Players were lured into the Baccarat pit, at the Roulette wheel, and in the Keno lounge. The most dangerous games of them all!*

Most of the noise was coming from the slot machines. Nearly 90,000 strong in Nevada. Earning millions for the casinos.

Didn't anyone realize the odds of hitting five 7's? It's $20 \times 20 \times 20 \times 20 \times 20$ to 1.** That's three-million two-hundred thousand to 1! Attractive? You've got to be kidding! About 50% of the gaming profits come from slots. No wonder.

It dawned on me that the great majority of players in that particular casino had no concept of the games. No understanding of odds and percentages. No awareness of the variations in game rules that can seriously hamper their ability to win.

Why don't they know?

Didn't anyone care?

I honestly believe the casinos could take all the aces out of the decks, and still pack the tables on Saturday night. I honestly believe that.

They could cram *ten* decks into the shoe, and few players would care. In Atlantic City, casinos use eight decks. Eight decks! Do you know the advantage that gives the casino?

Do you know a basic strategy for blackjack?

Do you know the variations in double-down rules?

Have you ever tried counting the cards?

Are you aware of a super-powerful count system, The Imperial Count, that's far and away the easiest to learn and play?

Do you know the difference between single and double-odds?

---

*CASINO ADVANTAGES: Keno-25% (or more), Slots-5-10%, Roulette-5.26%, Baccarat-1.59%, Craps-.63% (Pass-line/Double-odds), Blackjack-0% (with basic strategy).

**Based on five reels with twenty symbols, one "7" per reel.

Do you know the three bets to make at a dice table. That's right. Only three!

Do you know how to discipline yourself to make the right bets, find the right tables, play the right games, and quit winners?

Do you care, or do you just want to "make your donation" for another weekend?

P. T. Barnum put it best with the overly used adage, "There's a sucker born every minute." It's just that most of them hang around casinos!

Probably the same group that paid full sticker for their car, buys lottery tickets, invested in a bridge, and has three sets of encyclopedias at home.

These people aren't gambling. They're giving it away!

Anyone can learn how to win if they sincerely give a damn. If they can find the desire to stand up and challenge the casino. To break away from the passive crowd.

Give *Pay the Line* a few hours of your concentration. Then, your next visit to a casino will yield a radically different attitude about gambling.

You'll learn how to seek out only the most favorable playing conditions. How to discipline your play so that new strategies can work for you. How to play the games with a full understanding of the rules themselves, so that you know exactly what you're doing, why you're doing it, and what your chances really are to walk away a winner.

You'll instantly recognize the wrong moves you *would have made*. You'll have a new confidence based on skill. You can play proudly, knowing you're going to be damn tough to beat! And isn't that what it's really all about.

Pay the Line isn't hype. It's clout! And plenty of it. Start at the very beginning and read every word. Repeat any sections that you didn't fully understand. Invest an evening. And prepare yourself to win!

CHAPTER 1

WHAT WINNING REALLY MEANS

"Pay the Line" is an expression everyone loves to hear at the dice tables. The stickman is telling the dealers to pay the players, the dice passed, you win! Winning . . . winning at anything is an exciting experience and a feeling of confidence that goes far beyond monetary gain.

Everyone wants to win. No one wants the stigma of being a loser. The pure value of winning helps to explain why some people can be thrilled with a $20 win, an amount that's little more than a gratuity for others.

I can recall the days when winning $50 on a football game was totally satisfying. It made my weekend. In retrospect, it was the *win* that was satisfying. $50 wasn't going to change my lifestyle. The sheer pleasure was *picking the winner*! I felt as much a winner as the winning team I bet on.

It's important that you understand the psychology of this example because your attitudes and emotions play a critical role in winning, whether you win $50 or several thousand.

Over the years, I've taught myself to be happy with a win of any amount. It may be elementary, but you must appreciate the fact that winning any amount of money is much better than losing any amount of money. If the winning sessions are small, let them accumulate.

You must train yourself to be happy with a win of any amount, simply because it *is* a win. You're on the plus side of the ledger.

Remember that losses, especially those that follow winning sessions, can take a greater toll on your feelings, moods, and confidence levels, than the financial set-back to your billfold.

ARE YOU SERIOUS ABOUT WINNING?

Every weekend, thousands of players make their pilgrimage to Las Vegas, Reno, or Atlantic City for a "little" gambling, with the pretense of only losing two or three hundred dollars.

Like sheep being led to slaughter, they identify with, and spend more time thinking about losing (or at least limiting their losses) than forming an all-out attack to win.

Do they have a burning desire to win? Apparently not.

On that typical weekend, Los Angeles empties into Las Vegas, San Francisco migrates to Reno, and New York jams the Garden State Parkway to Atlantic City.

The casinos have turned on their magnet for another big slam. Believe this statistic . . . *over 95% of all the players are not skilled, have no serious plan to win, and honestly anticipate a loss.* Not surprisingly, they go home a loser.

It must be that most weekend gamblers simply like to play. Winning would be nice, but the real motivation is the fun and excitement of big-time gambling on that typical get-away weekend. They like the shows, the pools, and the lavish, relaxing atmosphere of a big casino. It's relaxing all right, like a shot of Demerol just before an operation. An operation to remove your wallet!

Do Casinos Always Win?

We'll cover the casinos specifically in a later chapter, but just in case you're not sure how well they do, listen to this. In the first six months of 1983, all nine Atlantic City casinos reported a gross win of $804,297,404! And that's purely gaming revenue. Not to mention other income from hotel operations. Oh, they win all right, and they win consistently over the long term.

Occasionally you'll hear about a big hotel in financial trouble. Don't for a moment think that someone hurt the place at the tables. The tables always win over the long term. If a hotel is showing a poor financial statement, it's usually a result of mismanagement, questionable investments, or start-up costs. *The tables are income they can count on*!

Do You Gamble for Entertainment?

Why make it easy for the casino to take your money. Spare me the silly excuse about counting your losses as a "cost for entertainment." If you're going to a casino with your hard-earned money, just to be entertained at the tables, you've got a screw loose, friend.

I suggest you read this book thoroughly, and consider *winning* for a change. But don't just consider it, attack it with all the skill and spirit you can assemble.

Preparation for Winning

Let's look at the more active gambler, who represents more than the weekend player. A player who may have actually developed a strategy. A player who's "casino-oriented" (as the bosses would call them) and may show above-average skill.

Chances are, the player's skill is limited to his count strategy at blackjack and a fair knowledge of craps, but little comprehension of odds.

He probably knows the best bet at craps is the pass-line, but does he know the right odds, and does he know the bets to stay away from?

At blackjack, he knows he must hit a 16 against the dealer's 10, but does he know the odds of making a pat hand?

Does he know that some casinos will allow him to "surrender" his cards, as he should do? Or does he think all the game rules are the same? *Playing rules vary significantly from one casino to another.*

What's more, this player is probably lacking a set of "personal" rules that only a handful of players actually establish. Obvious rules such as knowing when to quit a session (why is it that so many players never know when to quit); refusing to play under less than favorable conditions; knowing when to press your bets, and when not to.

What's missing, nine times out of ten, is the discipline to follow your own rules, if in fact you have any. The casinos have their own rules that are followed to the letter. You need your own set of rules also, and the discipline to make them work for you.

A New Definition for Winning

The next time you plan a trip to your favorite casino, consider a new definition for winning and losing. Winning is being *successful*; losing is being a *failure*. If you win, you succeed; if you lose, you fail.

Does it sound different? "Failing" sure sounds a lot worse than "losing" doesn't it. No one wants to fail; in business, in marriage, or in school. Those are scars no one wants.

But for some reason, failing in a casino is an *"accepted"* failure. We've all trained ourselves to accept a gambling loss because: "it's so difficult to win," or the classic, "it won't hurt me, I can handle it," and the famous, "it's just a cost of entertainment."

Do you enroll in college with the same apathetic outlook? Would you consider getting married with that same complacent attitude? Certainly not. Then why is a gambling failure any different?

Even for the small bettor, when you add up the losses over several years, you might be looking at several thousand, maybe tens of thousands of dollars. This is no time for apathy, let's get serious!

LEARN HOW TO ACCEPT A LOSS

Losses are inevitable. Some players can handle a loss from both the financial aspect and the emotional impact. Some can't. Don't think that all players are not affected "inside" by a particular loss. It happens to most everyone.

Guarding against it is simply accepting the fact that a loss now and then is bound to occur. I suggest you plan for it. Be prepared just in case. Make sure you can cope with it.

If you're typically a "bad" loser, gambling is a bad idea. You know how you react losing a tennis match, an account, or a big contract. That's the issue here. How do you deal with it? Do you act like an adult or a child? If you throw your club because you put the ball in the woods, first consider growing up, then consider gambling.

Sometimes, a gambling loss can cause much more than a short-term reaction to certain people. The frustrations may drift over into your everyday life at home and at work, putting a damper on just about everything, taking the polish off your otherwise enjoyable activities.

If this is a problem you can relate to, or you suspect it

could happen to you, the solution is not necessarily to stop gambling. Indeed, losses occur everywhere, every day, not just in casinos. Sure, I personally suggest you *do* stop gambling, but how do you stop the other losses that bring on the same consequences?

I'm not a psychiatrist, but I strongly believe that the best way to counter the damaging effects of a loss is *with a win*! Find things, or make things happen that represent a win to you.

Earlier, we referred to losing as a "failure" and to winning as a "success." Perhaps the real reason that losses (failures) gnaw at some people is a distinct absence of successes. If I lost all the time, I'd probably be in a bad mood too!

In baseball, when you score a run, it's a success; when the other team scores a run, it's a failure. At the end of nine innings, the team with the most runs is usually in the best mood. Score some runs!

I realize this book is about winning, and here we are talking about losing. How depressing. But without this vital preparation—knowing how to cope with a loss, we're not a complete player.

THE ADDICTIVE GAMBLER

On a recent golf outing, I played in a foursome with three of my best business customers, that quite frankly, I was trying to impress. I can usually break an 80, but on that particular day I played very poorly. I missed easy putts, drove the ball out-of-bounds at least five times, and even whiffed a tee-shot completely! Embarrassed? It was more than that. I felt like a complete loser! I'm sure my playing partners felt the same about me.

When you're on the golf course, your business fortunes mean nothing. Your game is what counts. I forgot that I'm a successful businessman. I forgot all the positive things that keep me going. All I could think about was shooting one of the worst rounds of my life, at the most inopportune time.

The disgust of playing like a weekend duffer grew bigger with every hole. Finally, on the 18th green, I had a chance to salvage the day with an easy par putt, no more than 3 feet from the hole. At least I could have ended the round on a high-note. When I walked up to the putt, I didn't study it for some reason. I didn't take any practice strokes as I usually do. I just hit it. The ball ran at least 10 feet beyond the cup. I then three-putted for a fat triple-bogey 7!

I putted the ball as if I didn't want to make it. As if I purposely wanted to miss my par. Why? Could it have been that I wanted to punish myself for playing such a lousy round? You bet it was! I missed that putt because I felt that I didn't deserve it.

And here's the kicker. Leading psychiatrists believe that compulsive gamblers continue to gamble for exactly the same reason. They *want* to lose! It's hard to believe, but they actually want to punish themselves for losing in the first place. Make sense? How could anyone purposely want to lose? It made sense in my golf story, why not in gambling.

Yes, it *is* the reason for compulsive gambling. Self-inflicted punishment. An urge to self-destruct. Now you know, if you didn't already, what really drives the compulsive gambler. It's an ugly addiction. I hope you never have to worry about it.

Tricks of the Mind

In case you still can't believe it, here's another example that might be closer to home.

Most people today are very concerned about their appearance. It seems that everyone exercises and jogs to keep fit and in shape. But what about people who are overweight? To some people, being thin is an obsession. They can't stand being fat!

Ever notice what happens sometimes, if they're provoked about their weight, or urged to diet by a friend? The sheer mention of their weight problem will bring on *more* eating! As if they're doing it to spite their friend. In fact, they're spiting themselves!

Some overweight people are depressed with their problem and ashamed of it deeply inside. Calling attention to it simply hits a nerve. Instead of dieting, they eat more, and you guessed it . . . to punish themselves for being overweight in the first place.

There's yet another reason for compulsive gambling that has come to light recently. It deals with the individual who is so straight, so perfect in everything, that it appears he has no failures! Perhaps he's a successful athlete, a star in sports. He doesn't drink, doesn't smoke. A perfect specimen. Get's all the girls. Know the type?

Gambling can put an end to this guy's misery. Yes, misery! Everyone is suppose to have a vice. No individual is allowed to be perfect. Gambling becomes an outlet for failure. It makes up for an otherwise impeccable life. He feels better.

Doesn't make a bit of sense does it? It's hard to figure. But the reasons we've just cited are medical fact. Tricks of the mind. Hopefully, one good way to put an end to this compulsion is to simply identify it. And that's what I've done.

QUESTIONS YOU MUST ANSWER

Before you wager a single silver dollar, ask yourself these important questions:

1. "Why do I want to Gamble?"
2. "Can I afford to?"

3. "Do I have a strong desire to win?"
4. Can I be satisfied with a small win?"

(1) If you're not sure why you want to gamble, don't even consider it. Your indecisiveness may be trying to tell you something. You must respond immediately to that question. Your answer must indicate a strong desire to win! Never gamble just for the fun of it.

(2) If there's reason to believe you can't really afford it, don't do it. There are no guarantees. If money's tight, and you're on limited income, why risk it?

(3) If you're not positively sure you seriously want to win, you probably won't. It's that simple. Part of winning is your attitude, which affects your preparation, commitment, discipline, and desire. It has to be there.

(4) Do you know what it means to quit winners? Can you say to yourself, "That's enough, I've got what I want, I can play again later"? If you're an average player with an average income, will $100 make you happy? Is that enough?

How Much is Enough?

If you're only interested in a big score, I urge you to stay out of casinos. You're a perfect example of the casino's "favorite player" . . . a victim of greed, the casino's biggest ally.

Don't get me wrong. There's nothing wrong with setting your sights high. I hope you win thousands and thousands of dollars! But, in the casino *you must have the ability to recognize an opportunity, and the wisdom to know that you can't force it to happen*. In the real world, you can make your own opportunities. In the casino, you can only look for them.

If you managed to win $200 during a brief "opportunity," why give it back looking for the big score when the opportunity has long vanished. Try it again later.

In the casino you must have the ability to recognize an opportunity, and the wisdom to know
that you can't force it to happen. In the real
world, you can make your own opportunities.
In the casino, you can only look for them.

CHAPTER 2

RULES OF DISCIPLINE

At first glance, this chapter may seem out of place. Logically, we would now begin to discuss the games in general and learn how to play with new, exciting strategies for you to enjoy. Not yet.

This chapter may very well be *the most important of the entire book*. Each sub-heading is a Rule of Discipline that you positively must respect, believe in, and abide by . . . without fail.

As you read the chapter, ask yourself, "Can I do this, do I believe it, do I understand why." If not, proceed no further.

There is little reason to learn new strategies to beat the casino, if you're going to shoot blanks. I'll teach you where to aim, give you the ammunition, but you are the player who ultimately pulls the trigger.

GREED IS A LOSER'S ALLY

We've already discussed in the opening chapter what winning must mean to you. Remember, winning must be reduced in your mind to its simplest terms—*if you have won any amount, you have not lost*! You must be content with a win of any amount.

Reverse psychology applies here. I'm not necessarily teaching you how to win, I'm teaching you how *not* to lose. Let small winning sessions accumulate. You'll be pleasantly surprised when you count up the chips.

This is not to say that every winning session will be small. You'll hit a big one from time to time, and more power to you!

The best teacher has experienced and remembers his own lessons. When I tell you to be happy with a small win, it's based on personal, unpleasant experiences. Years ago, a small win simply wasn't good enough for me. You've heard these horror stories time and time again.

I can vividly recall playing at the Desert Inn, late at night, up a few hundred, watching choppy dice, tired and ready for bed. I played on and on . . . looking for that hot hand that never came. I gave the few hundred back, little by little, wrote another marker, and lost that too. I could have quit winners, had a pleasant night's sleep, and looked forward to playing again the next day, sharp, alert, and ahead!

In stark contrast, I was down about as much as I had won at that critical time. Instead of leaving the casino, I stayed, as if my legs were chained to the tables. I wanted the big score, nothing less would satisfy me. Fortunately I've learned how to be content since those days with a win of any amount. *It's the first Rule of Discipline*—Greed is a Loser's Ally! Greed makes losers out of winners.

The Professional Gambler

There are honest-to-gosh professional gamblers who live in Nevada, play regularly, and win regularly. Unlike the Hollywood image you might conjure up of a real, professional gambler, you'll be surprised to learn that his initial bets are one, two, maybe three red chips ($5).

Bets of two or three silver dollars are not uncommon. He's looking for $40-$50 a day. $300 a week is realistic. He knows what can happen if he plunks down $500 on the first bet.

Usually, he plays blackjack and expertly counts the cards. But no one bothers him. He poses no grave threat to the casino. He grinds out his secure, satisfying profit through disciplined play. Is he greedy? Not on your life! To a professional, "greed" is a cancerous term that has no place in his vocabulary.

Slot Machines

Slot machines bring out the greed in players more than any other casino game. Many slots today provide frequent payouts on a "hold" of less than 3%. In addition, new "progressive" video machines offer large jackpots in the hundreds of thousands of dollars!

Those large jackpots may at first appear to be too expensive for a casino to offer. In fact, the jackpots work on a player's greed, pulling every last silver dollar out of their pocket.

Few players are satisfied with a win of $50, or bars across for $100. Invariably, those winnings and the original stake are dumped right back into the machine to line up five 7's, the big score, a one in three-million shot at the moon.

A casino executive told me recently that the big progressive machines actually generate greater profits than the more basic machines in spite of the huge payouts.

Why, because most all players give these machines *all their money*. Few players quit when they're ahead. They go strictly for the big jackpot which is virtually the same as going for broke!

I mention slots purely as an example of greed. I don't recommend playing them. If you must play and justify the expense as entertainment, consider that for the same entertainment investment, you could have easily dined in the casino's finest gourmet restaurant, or taken in a nice show. Isn't that a more sensible way to spend your "entertainment" money?

Remember, *slots are for greedy losers*.

MANAGE YOUR MONEY WISELY

I'm sure you've noticed the player who walks up to a Blackjack table and asks for a thousand in chips. His first bet is $500. Everyone else at the table watches his hand with more interest than their own. You probably are impressed with this guy.

When I see a player do this, I assume he has money coming out of his ears, and his brains are right behind. No one in his right mind begins play with a large bet. It defeats every plausible rule of betting.

The casinos love this kind of player. That should tell you something. He is a typical "comped" player who loses nine times out of ten, giving generously to the casino. Too bad he doesn't give this money to the Cancer Society, an orphan's fund, or send it home to his mother. What a philanthropist!

How the hell can a player who is obviously successful in business, play so ill-prepared, with such unnecessary risk. God help him if he runs his business that way.

The first rule of money management is to *bet safely in the beginning of each session to protect against sudden and unpredictable losses*. Don't be wiped out before you've even seen the pool.

My initial bet at a crap table is always $15, 3 red chips. This represents a "3-unit bet" which allows for special odds that we will describe fully in a later chapter on craps. At the blackjack tables, I rarely begin with more than a $15 bet, 3 red chips.

The Value of a Dollar

Let's make comparisons between my meager $15 opening bet and the highroller's $500. If you would ask the big bettor why he begins so strongly with large bets, his answer would probably be that $500 to him is about the same as $15 might be to you and me (an equalizer in earnings and lifestyle).

There are serious flaws in that reasoning. $500 is exactly $500 in his pocket, my pocket, or your pocket. $500 buys a nice wardrobe, a television, or fine patio furniture for all of us. It's a lot of money! Period!

Incidentally, money values tend to depreciate when you're gambling. And quickly restored when you get home. Here's another important rule of money management. *Never put two different values on the same dollar.* Be sure you fully respect the constant value of money.

Bet Safely and Keep Your Winnings!

I have nothing against a $500 bet. In fact, I often make bets that are much more. And I hope you do also when the time is opportune.

But, never begin play with such a large bet. You haven't tested the waters, and you may be risking all or substantially all of your stake.

Do however, find the guts to make these large bets when you are substantially up, winning the great majority of your hands, and following precise betting strategies that we will cover in the chapter specifically on betting.

Can you see the important difference in when to make the big bet? There's little risk betting a large bet when you're up 4 or 5 times the size of the bet. You're betting back a portion of your winnings against the house.

Casinos consider this type of play dangerous. You're giving them a good shot at your *small bets*, then beating them over the head with the *big ones*. Relentlessly, you play them tough. A smart bettor!

Always follow this cardinal rule of betting. *Start small, press up 30 to 50% of your bet when you're winning with consistency; lay back or walk away when you're losing.* Never . . . repeat, never press up during a losing session.

There are times more frequent than you might imagine when you are well ahead during a typical playing session. Set aside some of those winnings by putting the chips in your pocket, give them to your wife or your girlfriend, but get them off the table and out of your sight. It's analogous to putting money in the bank. This practice will insure that you *quit winners*!

Play the few chips you have left, and try to build them up to a new plateau. Quit if you lose them.

Casinos hate the player who puts chips in his pocket. By doing so, you've ruined their shut-out. You've already chalked one up in the win column. You continue to play without pressure. You know you've beaten them!

PLAY WHEN IN OPTIMUM CONDITION

A friend of mine, who goes to Vegas regularly, always comes back a loser. He hurries to the hotel, has the valet park the car, checks in, and literally stumbles over his luggage to get to the nearest crap table. No time to wind down from the long flight, no time to relax. This is a story that really doesn't have to be finished. You can write your own ending.

Visitors to Nevada are rarely conditioned for play as the locals who live there. There's a certain anxiety upon arrival. An urge to play that must be tempered. A schedule is important, but it must be followed.

I never play until the evening of the day I arrive, and only then if I'm mentally prepared, rested, and cautiously optimistic.

It should be obvious, but it needs to be said. *Play only when you're relaxed, in good spirits, alert, and with a clear mind.* Indeed, why play when you're tired, rushed, tentative, annoyed, or bothered with a problem. It's going to cost you. You can count on it!

I strongly believe in gut feelings . . . instinct, whatever you want to call it. Unknown senses alert me that I'm heading for trouble, making a mistake. If I'm getting that signal . . . a bad vibe, I won't play. I suggest that you respond to that kind of feeling as I do.

If you think you're about to lose, you probably will. If something tells you not to keep playing . . . stop!

I plan my sessions carefully. As a general rule, I prefer to play in the evening. A time when cocktail waitresses roam the casino touting free drinks. I like Scotch and water, but "Coke is it" when I'm gambling. I would never work in my office less than sober. Gambling is certainly no different. Since my sessions are frequent (I like to hit and run), there's plenty of time for a drink in the lounge, or a break in the coffee shop.

The Last Day of the Trip

There's a particular segment of your trip that demands the utmost caution. The day you fly home. Believe me, the last day must be judiciously reckoned with.

How many times do you suppose, the last day in the casino turned into disaster. The average player has a tendency to bet with reckless abandon in an effort to recoup losses, get even, maybe win a little.

Even if you're up going into the final morning, there's a likelihood you'll think to yourself, "God, I won't be back here for another 6 months, a year, whatever." "I'll play just another few hundred, that's all."

In that statement, "play" is a euphemism for "lose." Think about it. What you're really thinking is, "I'll lose no more than just another few hundred, that's my limit."

You might think that a little more gambling will help to get it out of your system for a while. Many players will skip breakfast that morning to get in an extra half-hour at the tables. If you're ahead, you theorize that you can't get hurt. If you're down, an obsession to get even throws discipline to the wind.

I purposely ask my travel agent to schedule my return flight for an early departure, 7 a.m. or so. If there's a red-eye available, I'll be on it. The night before I leave is my last playing session. The polls have closed. The next time I play will be the first evening of my next trip.

It's 10 a.m. and your plane leaves at noon! Never, repeat, never play when you're rushed.

USE COMMON SENSE

At one time, I gave most of my play to the Desert Inn in Las Vegas. Compared to other strip hotels, the "DI" is relatively small (800 rooms), but there's a distinctly warm ambience in the casino, and a relaxing club atmosphere on the grounds that I totally enjoyed.

Today, I play in numerous casinos paying careful attention to "house rules" that vary from one casino to another. We'll cover that important subject later in the chapter on casinos.

Anyhow, an incident at the Desert Inn comes to mind that is the perfect example of using common sense. I was walking around the blackjack tables, playing green chips, looking for a good spot to sit down.

I noticed one table that had just emptied. The dealer was an attractive lady, so I figured why not. She looked at me as

I settled in as if to say "do you really want to play at this table?" I kidded her about losing all her customers, and asked if she took all their money. Her succinct response has stuck in my mind ever since. "I'm strong," she said. "No one's beaten me all day."

Like a dummy, I played through the shoe and watched her turn over 19's, 20's, and 21's to no end. She dealt me those great 15's and 16's that seemed to bust everytime I took a hit. I limped through the shoe and figured I'd get a fresh shuffle and turn this thing around. The second shoe was the same damn thing, pat hands for her, and stiffs for me.

The dealer has no control over how the cards come up. If a monkey could deal the cards, it wouldn't make any difference. I knew she felt sorry. She reminded me about the warning before I sat down. Why the hell didn't I listen to her!

The moral to this story is simple. If a dealer tells you she's strong . . . believe it! Common sense tells you to try another table. Even to this day, I always ask the dealer when I sit down if she's (or he's) strong.

I recommend that before you choose a table, stand by for a few hands and watch the outcome. Notice the chips in the dealer's till and in front of the players. Who's winning? Above all, remember to do as I do; ask the dealer, "Are you strong?" I have no reason to expect anything but a straight answer to that important question.

Don't Get Cocky

After a big winning session, a player has a tendency to get cocky. He remembers all those place bets he hit at the dice table, and those three 21's in a row at blackjack. "Hell, this is easy!"

Well, things change, my friend. Dice are capricious, and cards turn faster than the Indy 500. A cocky player who thinks he can't lose is in for a big and sudden surprise. You'll lose it back in a tenth of the time you won it. That fast! You might be formidable, but you're not infallible.

Develop a Business Attitude

As you can appreciate, common sense and keen discipline are assets to everyday living, including gambling. Then why do you suppose the most conservative, staunch, successful businessmen leave it all behind on their way to Atlantic City?

They play as if they just wanted to have some fun on the weekend, make their "donation" (I hate that phrase), and get back to serious business on Monday.

What *isn't* serious about losing money in Atlantic City? Is it OK to lose in an Atlantic City casino as long as you win in a Manhattan office building? I guess it all depends on whether you simply want to play, or you really want to win.

The analogy of gambling to business is indeed appropriate. Treat your gambling as you would your own enterprise. For many players, the casino is *their* office, a place to do business.

My most recent trip to Vegas was with three business associates. After our first blackjack session, we had a lot to talk about. What did we do? We went to the lounge and had a business meeting . . . about blackjack! We discussed what had just happened, made decisions, corrections, and revamped our plan.

We treated the tables like a business venture. Not surprisingly, we all won that trip, one of us substantially!

I'm not suggesting you only play in three-piece vested suits, although quite honestly, I seem to play better in a suit and tie than in blue jeans and sneakers. I feel like an executive instead of a lowly tourist. Try it.

The comparison of gambling and business can't be overstated. In my office, I tackle a business problem by first getting all the information . . . not half-answers. I make a decision based on logical, judicial, common sense. Sometimes it's a gut-instinct, but I'll always back it up. I clear my mind, weigh all the information, throw out any bias, and make my decision.

I would never, for example, issue a new price schedule without first checking internal costs and what my market will allow. I don't release a new product without first doing a market study, to find out what the market wants, and what the market already has. I don't make a move in my business until I've checked and rechecked data on which to base an important decision. I gamble the same way.

The Competitive Spirit to Succeed

Incidentally, the drive you need to reach success, to accomplish your goals, is a persistive, competitive spirit. Are you competitive? Can you respond enthusiastically to a challenge, see it through, and win? Or is it just going to lay there. Hopefully, you're as competitive by nature as I am, in the casino, on the tennis courts, anywhere. Get the spirit and give it your best shot!

"Far better it is to
dare mighty things,
to win glorious
triumphs, even
though checkered
with failure, than to
take rank with those
poor spirits who
neither enjoy much
nor suffer much,
because they live
in the grey twilight
that knows not
victory nor defeat."

THEODORE ROOSEVELT

NEVER BUCK A TREND

Let's say you've read in the sports section that the White Sox are on a 12-game tear. They've won 12 in a row, and 15 of their last 16 games. You've studied the pitchers and you've looked at the line. Now what do you do?

You either bet the Sox or you pick another game! Here's a rule that you'll be tested on in the casino time and time again. *Never buck a trend*!

If you've won ten hands in a row at blackjack, continue pressing up. Don't lay back. I've heard insane reasons for jumping out of a streak.

"I can't believe I'm going to win another hand."

"A loss is going to fit in right about here somewhere."

"I'm up a bunch, just in case I lose the next hand, I'll pull back some chips."

It's all foolish reasoning. Thinking that way, you'll never need the proverbial tray to carry all your chips to the cashier.

Chapter 8 outlines specific betting strategies based on pressing bets at precisely determined increments, during a streak. We give you two schedules, one for the small bettor, and another for the player who is willing to risk more initially. Following our strategy for the small bettor, you would have won nearly a thousand on a ten-hand streak, while putting only a modest stake in jeopardy.

Convince yourself at this moment, that you'll never let a streak of that magnitude slip by. Remember, *bet with the streak, never against it*.

DON'T PLAY ON CREDIT

Casinos make it as easy as possible for you to lose your money. Most of the big hotels are so lavish, with big pools, the finest suites, gourmet restaurants, golf courses, spas, elegance that boggles the mind. And that's precisely the intention. This kind of setting is certainly more conducive to free-spending than in your neighbor's kitchen on poker night.

It's a lot easier to lose money while being fanned by lovely maidens feeding you grapes. I'm not sure if that's available, but if you look for it in Vegas you'll probably find it.

This brings us to casino credit. Yes, credit. Just like your charge account at Sears. With credit, you can write markers and play, and play, and play, until it's all gone. Wow, that's fun!

And credit in a casino is very easy to get. You fill out an application for credit no different than any other credit form. Information is provided including, and most important of all, your bank name and checking account number. The casino credit manager will call your bank to learn your average daily balance.

That's important, because when credit is issued to you in chips, you must sign a marker. A marker is not an I.O.U. It's not a receipt. It's not a bill. It's a real check!

The fine print on the "check" says that you agree not to stop payment, and that you allow the casino to fill in any missing information such as your checking account number.

Gaming Commission rules state that a casino must deposit the check within 45 days, if you have not by then made good on it. Generally, most credit players pay on receipt of a statement with their own personal check. In a few days, the casino will return the original marker.

Casino markers are now considered legally enforceable. If the marker is presented to your bank, and it bounces, I suggest you make satisfactory arrangements. No one will break your leg if you don't pay up, but you can expect to hear from a collection agency working for the casino.

The pitfall of credit is simple. It's too damn easy to ask for a thousand! Here's the situation. You're out of chips, the table's cold, you should walk away. But, you look at the pit boss, hold up five fingers, and before you can breathe, the dealer shoves over $500, or $5,000, depending on how much your fingers are worth. Now, wasn't that easy. Another $500, big deal. It's a big deal back in Pleasantville, Ohio, but in Vegas? Who's counting?

The Casino "Comp"

When you get credit at a casino, the next logical thing to do is try to get comped. "Comped" means you have received a complimentary "gift" from the casino, such as a free room, a free show, maybe free air-fare.

I get a kick out of the first chapter of a popular book on gambling, that tells how easy it is to get a free trip to Vegas . . . lots of freebees. Nothing's free, my friend. Don't be misled.

The cheapest comp is usually a "free" show in the main room. Big deal! It probably cost you $100 at the craps tables to get the free show!

Another cheap comp is called a "casino-rate" on the room. All hotels have a "commercial" rate they offer to airlines, travel agents, convention groups, etc., which is usually about half the regular room-rate.

To the inexperienced gambler, who just got some neat credit, a casino-rate on the room is usually taken for granted. If his credit line is under $2,500, that's about all he can expect.

To get the casino-rate, you must play at least one green chip, consistently and frequently. As with most comps, the pressure to make the bets to "qualify" ends up costing you more at the tables than the savings on the room. It's a farce!

If you want the better rate, get it from your travel agent! Depending on the time of year, most all casinos offer at least one or two special "packages."

Comps of any value are strictly for the highrollers. You

know, the guys who start out big with the black chips. C_
sinos love the player who immediately bets with both fists!

They hate the player who bets cautiously at first to learn
the drift of the table. The guy who puts only small wagers
in jeopardy is not going to get comped. If he presses hard
when he's winning, betting the casino's losses right back at
them, you can be assured he's not the kind of player the
casino will comp.

Put another way, he's not the kind of player *the casino
wants*!

I firmly believe both credit and comps are for losers. Credit
may be convenient (you bet it is), and the comps are attractive, but think hard about why you're really getting it.

Comp Criteria

How does a casino decide whether or not to give you a
comp? This is probably the most misunderstood element of
gambling I know of. Few people really understand the comp
scene. Let's analyze it.

When you write a marker, immediately a floorman or pit
boss will watch you play. I say "immediately" because your
first bet is noted. The amount of your first few bets is important in determining the potential of earnings from your
play. Secondly, the length of time you played, and the average bet size over the session is recorded. Whether you win
or lose is somewhat incidental. What they really want to
know is *how much money did you put in jeopardy and for
how long*, in the event you did lose.

The amount of your first few bets carries a lot of weight
in making a comp consideration. Not surprisingly, the casino
wants to see large bets. And if that's what they want, do you
really suppose that's what you should do to win? Isn't it
obvious by now?

At the end of the session, the boss may grade your play.

Someone eventually will. You'll get a grade of good, fair, or poor. If your rating is "good," it doesn't mean you're a good player, it means you're a good player *for the casino*!

Remember the highrollers we talked about with the hundred-grand cards? Rest assured they get air-fare, first-class for two, a nice suite, din-din, and much more. Some of these guys don't give a damn if they lose fifty-thousand! It's not unusual for a player to lose millions of dollars at the bacarrat tables in just two or three nights.

My days of playing on credit are far behind me. No longer do I put up with the intimidation of being watched and graded. Compelled to impress a pit boss for comp consideration.* Win or lose, I'm playing at my own pace, making any size bet I damn well want to.

I especially like the fact that playing with cash puts an absolute limit on my losses. You can't play your Rolex at the dice tables. I win considerably more times than I lose, but when that inevitable loser is a reality, I want to know exactly what's in my pocket, not what's left in the computer at numerous hotels.

For another reason, I like playing anonymously. Most often, when I'm at a table no one knows my name, my credit, or where I bank. When I win, only I know it. It may not be for you, and that's fine. The great majority of play (in terms of money, not players) today is on credit.

Incidentally, the few players who are a serious threat to a casino are rarely comped, and may in fact be barred from play entirely. The courts are undecided on the rights of a casino to bar a player. Recent lower court rulings have been for the player, but have allowed certain casino countermea-

---

*The only comp I get anymore is a VIP pass to avoid the long lines waiting to see a show. Usually, any appreciable "action" at the tables deserves the "pass." Just ask any pit boss for a "line-pass" while (not after) you're playing.

sures such as bet-limiting and random shuffling to stifle the expert counter.

I'll end this chapter with one last pleading. When you're playing on credit, and expecting a comp, you've got two strikes against you.

The Casino's Viewpoint

A pit boss at a big strip hotel, and a long-time friend of mine, had a chance to scan my Rules of Discipline before going to press. It seemed important at the time to get the other side's reaction. "A damn nice job," he said, "and I've read a lot of these."

He showed no concern, but I didn't expect any. I don't (and he doesn't) expect an army of players marching into his casino with my book tucked under their arms.

He made another good point . . . "No one can teach people not to be greedy." "Hell, I've got players with hundred-grand cards (credit line) who would be bored silly betting 15 bucks." He's absolutely right!

He knew, however, that I hit the casino's comp program dead-center. But he wasn't worried that anyone would cancel their credit. Having credit in Vegas is some sort of status symbol. The bigger the credit, the more diamonds in the ring.

If you're one of the highrollers with a hundred-grand card, you play your money, and I'll play mine. Go get 'em tiger!

CHAPTER 3

CRAPS, HOW TO PLAY

The casual observer in a casino, who knows little if anything about casino games, would pick craps as the most complicated, difficult-to-learn game. Why? Because the table layout *looks* complicated. There are so many different types of bets. So much confusion. Sometimes 7 wins, and sometimes it loses. Unfortunately, many gamblers shy away from craps because they assume it's too difficult to master.

As any experienced dice player knows, the game is indeed simple. Perhaps the easiest to learn and play. More importantly, it's the most exciting game in the casino. But most important of all, craps offers certain wagers that give the house only a slight advantage. Most of the "best" bets you can make in a casino are at the dice table.

To understand the game, let's first consider the dice. There are two dice in play, with each cube having six sides, 1 through 6. That means that numbers from 2 through 12 can appear when two dice are thrown.

Let's make an important distinction right now. The probability of each number varies. They are not all the same.

Your chances of rolling a 4 are much less than rolling a 7. We'll get into that in specific detail later in this chapter, but for now, it's important that you realize this fact from the outset.

COURTESY: DESERT INN, LAS VEGAS.

THE PASS-LINE BET

Let's list the numbers somewhat out-of-order, so you can best see what the numbers mean for the most common dice wager—the "pass-line" bet. Here are the numbers in groups for you to study. Always think of the numbers exactly as I've separated them.

2-3-12	7-11	4-10	5-9	6-8
Craps (loser)	Natural (winner)	Point Numbers (must be repeated to win)		

Each of the numbers: 2, 3, and 12 is called a "craps," and it's a loser. 7 and 11 are called a "natural," and it's a winner. The remaining numbers: 4, 5, 6, 8, 9, and 10 are called "point-numbers," and must be *repeated* before a 7 is rolled in order to win.

When a player is handed the dice to throw, the first roll is called a "come-out," and a 7 or 11 immediately wins. The 2, 3, or 12 immediately loses. If the player throws any of the other numbers: 4, 5, 6, 8, 9, or 10 . . . there is no decision yet.

The player continues to throw the dice until either that same point-number is rolled again (in which case the player wins), or until a 7 is rolled (in which case the player loses). Any other number has no significance to the pass-line wager.

Now you can see why the 7 sometimes wins, and sometimes loses. If it's thrown on the first roll, it wins. But if it's thrown while the player is trying to repeat his point-number, the 7 loses. And that's called a "seven-out."

The dice then pass to the next player, and it's his turn to shoot. As long as the shooter continues to make passes (wins), either on the come-out immediately with a 7 or 11, or by repeating the point successfully, he retains the dice. The player keeps the dice even if he loses on the come-out roll with a 2, 3, or 12. The player only loses the dice when he sevens-out.

What we've just described is a pass-line bet, the heart of craps, and the most widely made bet at the table.

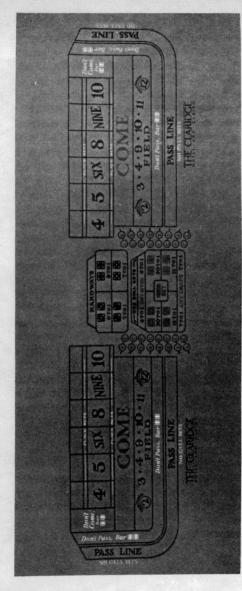

This is an exact replica of a modernized table layout, provided by the Claridge Hotel and casino in Atlantic City. Notice that the new layout gives the correct odds expressions for the prop bets, such as 7 to 1, instead of 8 "for" 1, long considered a deceitful tactic on older style layouts.

In addition, the new design does not include the big 6 or 8 on the corners, a bet that might become extinct be-

cause of its poor percentages, especially when compared to the corresponding place bet for the same numbers.

Other bets becoming increasingly unpopular among skilled players are the one-roll propositions such as any-7 and field bets. Since field bets appeal to the inexperienced player, giving over 5½% to the house, they are not recommended or discussed in this text.

Now, let's pretend to walk up to the table. Look at the illustration of the table layout. Notice the area marked "Pass-Line." That's where the pass-line wager is made. Place your bet in that part of the pass-line area that's *directly in front of you*.

Also notice that the pass-line extends around both ends of the table. And notice that in fact, both ends of the table are identical. For now, don't pay any attention to the rest of the layout.

Follow the "Puck"

How do you know if the shooter is "coming-out" or trying to repeat his point-number? It's easy. The first thing to notice on the table is a round 3¾" diameter "puck" that says "ON" on one side, and "OFF" on the other. The "ON" side is white, and the "OFF" side is black. Where this puck is located will tell you the stage of the game when you walk up.

Look at the table illustration again, and notice the big boxes at the back of the table that represent point-numbers. There's a set of boxes for both ends of the table. There's a box for the 4, 5, 6, 8, 9, and 10. If the shooter made a point on the come-out roll, and is now trying to repeat that number, that's where the dealers will place the puck. Towards the rear center of the correct box.

When the puck is placed in one of the point boxes, the white side (ON) is up. If the puck is in the box marked "six," that's the point-number the shooter is after.

If the puck is noticed with the black side (OFF) showing, it's usually placed in an adjacent box marked "Don't-Come," and that means the next roll is a come-out.

In Northern Nevada, the don't-come box is in a different spot for some reason, so the puck is placed directly beside (not in) the point box nearest to the end of the table. The puck is nearest to the 4-box on the left side of the table, and nearest to the 10-box on the right side.

As you might imagine, it usually takes more time for a shooter to try and repeat a point-number than to throw a craps or natural on the come-out roll. So, at that instant you walk up to the table, the shooter will probably be going for his point-number. Possibly, you timed it perfectly and the shooter is about to make his come-out roll.

That's your signal to make a pass-line wager. Incidentally, never make a pass-line bet while the shooter is trying for a point, because then it's a bad bet. We'll tell you why later in the chapter.

When the shooter wins, everyone on the pass-line wins! Unlike "street" craps, all the players at the dice table are playing against the house, not each other.

YOU MUST KNOW THE ODDS!

The next bet we must learn is called an "odds-bet," and it's directly associated with the pass-line bet that we now know how to make. But before we can understand the odds-bet, we have to learn what "odds" means, and what the correct odds are at a dice table for all the possible numbers. Study the following chart for a moment, and you'll soon learn the probability of rolling any particular number.

NUMBER	WAYS	PROBABILITY	HOW
2	1	35 to 1	1-1
3	2	17 to 1	1-2, 2-1
4	3	11 to 1	2-2, 1-3, 3-1
5	4	8 to 1	1-4, 4-1, 2-3, 3-2
6	5	6.2 to 1	3-3, 2-4, 4-2, 1-5, 5-1
7	6	5 to 1	1-6, 6-1, 2-5, 5-2, 3-4, 4-3
8	5	6.2 to 1	4-4, 2-6, 6-2, 3-5, 5-3
9	4	8 to 1	3-6, 6-3, 4-5, 5-4
10	3	11 to 1	5-5, 4-6, 6-4
11	2	17 to 1	5-6, 6-5
12	1	35 to 1	6-6
	36		

In this chart, it's readily apparent that there are more ways to roll a 7 than any other number. "Probability" means the same as odds, and it's easy to compute if you have to.

We know there are 36 ways to roll the dice. And we know there are six ways to roll a 7. That means there must be 30 ways to *not* roll a 7 (36−6). So our odds of rolling the seven are 30 to 6. Dividing both numbers by 6 gives us 5 to 1.

THE ODDS OF ROLLING A 7:

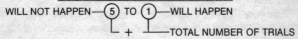

WILL NOT HAPPEN—(5) TO (1)—WILL HAPPEN
└ + ──────TOTAL NUMBER OF TRIALS

Out of six rolls, one roll should be a 7; five rolls should be some other number. *That's 5 to 1 odds.* Notice that I said "should be." It's not an absolute. It's an absolute probability.

The actual results may deviate somewhat over the *short-term*, and that's what a skilled player is looking for. *An opportunity when the odds have wavered.* But, over the *long-term*, a 7 will come up once for every six rolls. Never argue with the laws of probability.

Who Has the Advantage?

Now that we understand odds at the dice table, let's go back to the pass-line rules and see how we stand. Let's see who has the advantage.

OK, we know there are four ways to throw a craps, and eight ways to make a 7 or 11. Wait a minute! We have an edge here! You bet we do! The player always has a strong advantage on the come-out roll.

There must be a catch. And there is. The point-numbers! When the shooter has established a point, the casino gets the edge. Again, it's easy to see why.

There are six ways to make the 7, and remember the 7 loses when a point-number has been established. No other point-number can be made *six* ways. Your best chance of rolling a point-number before a 7 is obviously a 6 or 8, since both numbers can be made *five* ways. But the 7 is more likely.

That's why we said earlier never to make a pass-line bet when the shooter has established a point-number. That's a dumb bet! You're giving up the best part of a pass-line wager—the come-out roll where you have an edge, and you're getting down just at the time when the casino gets the nod. Not too smart!

The next logical question is who has the edge when you take *both* the come-out and point-numbers into account? Not surprisingly, the casino still gets the prize, but not by much. The casino advantage all-total, is 1.41%.

A Problem for You to Solve

The best way to fully grasp the probabilities of dice is to work out a problem on your own. Let me give you an easy problem to work on, all by yourself, and with the aid of our Probability Chart.

What are the odds that a shooter will throw a point-number on the come-out roll? Your answer will yield an important probability to always remember.

Now, find a piece of paper, a pencil, and work out the solution. In case you're too lazy to go look for a piece of paper, I'm instructing our printer to leave the rest of this page blank for a work area. You'll have to provide your own pencil. But, I'll only give you five minutes. That's all the longer I'll wait. Get going.

Done? What did you get? You better have figured *1 to 2*, or you flunk? Here's how we find it. We know there are 36 ways to roll the dice, right? And all the ways to throw only a point-number are 24.

POINT NUMBERS	WAYS EACH	TOTAL WAYS
6 & 8	5	10
5 & 9	4	8
4 & 10	3	6
		24

If we subtract the number of ways to make a point-number, 24, from the total ways for all numbers, 36, we have 12 . . . which obviously is the total number of ways *not* to make a point-number. So, 12 to 24 is easily reduced to 1 to 2. That's our answer!

Give yourself an "A" if you got it right. If you figured it out in your head because (a) you couldn't find a pencil, or (b) you didn't want to mess up the book, give yourself an "A+."

ODDS EXPRESSED AS A PERCENTAGE

When odds are expressed as 1 to 2, it means that in three trials to make an event happen, one time it won't happen, and two times it will. If we wish to express the odds as a percentage, as is often done, we simply divide the number of times the event *will happen* according to the odds, by the total number of trials (the total of both numbers in the odds expression).

In this case, we divide 2 by 3. That's the fraction 2/3 (fractions are still another way to express probabilities) and a percentage of 66%. *A 66% chance that our shooter will indeed make a point-number on the come-out roll.*

1 TO 2 ODDS EXPRESSED AS A FRACTION, NUMBER, PERCENTAGE:

$$\frac{\text{NUMBER OF TIMES AN EVENT WILL HAPPEN}}{\text{TOTAL NUMBER OF TRIALS *}} = \frac{2}{3} = .666 = 66.6\%$$

*The total of both numbers in the odds expression.

Yet a third way to express a probability, and technically we've already performed it, is with a number between 0 and 1. If an event can't possibly happen, the number is 0. If the event is positively bound to happen, the number is 1. In between are all the decimal numbers such as .666 (nothing more than the fraction expressed as a decimal).

You'll be happy to know that there are no other ways to express a probability that I know of. If there are any, I don't want to hear about it.

Readers who are learning from "scratch" may accuse me of writing a "trick" question, because the numbers appear to be turned around. Always remember that the first number represents the event *not happening*. Based on the way I purposely phrased the question, the answer of 1 to 2 is correct.

The first number (1), is smaller than the second number (2), because the odds are greater than even (1 to 1) that the event *will* happen.

If the likelihood of the event happening is less than even, as is more often the case, then the odds are obviously expressed with the larger number first.

If the question would have been phrased, "What are the odds that a shooter *will not* throw a point-number on the come-out roll," then the correct answer would have been 2 to 1, because the likelihood of the shooter *not* making a point-number is less than even.

Always Remember Point-Numbers in Pairs

You should now be able to see why we combined the point-numbers in our earlier chart . . . 6&8, 5&9, 4&10. Because the ways are the *same* for both numbers in each pair. Accordingly, when odds are computed for any point-number, it's always the same for the corresponding number in the pair.

Remember the point-numbers in pairs. That's important.

THE ODDS-BET

Now that we really understand odds, we can learn how to make the important odds-bet. This wager is made only when the shooter has established a point. Place the odds-bet directly behind the pass-line bet, but out of the pass-line area. The casino will allow you to bet an amount equal to your pass-line wager (single-odds) or double the amount of your pass-line bet if double-odds are offered. We'll see later in this chapter that double-odds is a big advantage to the player, so look for the casino that offers it.

What's nice about the odds-bet is that the casino will pay you correct odds on that bet, as opposed to the pass-line wager that pays even money (1 to 1).

Here's a chart that gives you the correct odds of the point-numbers being repeated before a 7 is rolled. It's important that you *remember these odds* because it tells you how you will be paid if you win.

POINT NUMBER	CORRECT ODDS OF REPEATING BEFORE A 7
6-8	6 to 5
5-9	3 to 2
4-10	2 to 1

Let's say the shooter established 4 as his point. If you have $5 bet on the pass-line, you can make an odds-bet of $5 (or $10 at a double-odds table). If the shooter successfully repeats the 4, you will be paid $5, even money, for the pass-line bet of $5, and 2 to 1 for your $5 odds-bet which is $10! (or $20 if you took $10 double-odds).

Since the casino pays off the odds-bet at correct odds, *there is absolutely no casino advantage*. In fact, the odds-bet is the only bet you can make in the casino that can be determined mathematically to have no advantage either to the player or to the casino. Over the long term, you'll neither win nor lose on your odds-bet wagers.

It's easy to prove that the odds-bet is indeed a fair bet. If the odds are 2 to 1 that a 7 will be rolled before a 4, then the payoff is correct, and the bet yields no advantage to the casino or player. We can compute from the earlier chart in this chapter that there are six ways to roll a 7, and three ways to roll a 4. 6 to 3 reduces to 2 to 1. Since the casino pays off at 2 to 1, they have no advantage.

Logically, you might ask why make such a big deal about a bet that only "evens out" over a long term. Let me answer your question with my own question. Would you rather make bets that *always* give the casino a rock-solid advantage, or would you prefer a bet that's truly a fair game? A bet in the casino that doesn't favor the house, *is* a big deal!

The Odds-Bet Reduces the Casino Advantage

Making the odds-bet along with the pass-line wager reduces the casino's total pass-line advantage from 1.4% to about .85%. Double-odds reduces the house edge even more to about .63%! True, you're risking more money to earn a lower house percentage, but it's strongly recommended.

Although the double-odds bet does not directly affect the house percentage on the pass-line part of the wager, it does lower the percentage for the *total amount of your wager.* And in reality, that's what we're concerned about.

The key to using double-odds sensibly is in the way you "size" your bets. Let's compare a pass-line wager of $15 with no odds to another pass-line bet of $5 with $10 in odds. If the point is 4, you would be paid only $15 in winnings for the $15 pass-line wager, compared to $25 for the $5 pass-line bet with $10 odds. See? It depends on how you structure your bets to earn the advantage of double-odds without increasing your total risk.

The Odds-Bet Must be a Proper Amount

Most players have little difficulty understanding single or double-odds, and regularly make the odds-bets as they should.

The problem usually comes in betting the proper amount in order to be paid correctly. Here's an example.

If the player has a $5 line bet and the point-number is 5, it seems perfectly proper to make a $5 odds-bet, right?

Wrong! How can the casino correctly pay off the odds-bet if it wins? 3 to 2 odds means the casino will pay $3 to every $2 wagered. Two goes into $5 two and a half times, multiplied times three is $7.50. A bit elementary but that's the way to think it through.

But, there are no half-dollars at the crap tables! A silver dollar (or $1 chip) is the smallest they have. *Always make sure the payoff is possible for the casino using $1 as the minimum divisible value.*

I know, some "downtown" casinos have 25 cent chips and you play all day for a dollar. I can get that kind of action at home watching "Gilligan's Island"! This book is at least for the $2 bettor, so we're assuming a $2 minimum table.

But what if you only wanted to bet $5 on the line? That's fine. If the point is 5 or 9, the casino will allow you to increase your odds-bet wager to $6. You'll get 3 to 2 for your $6 which correctly pays off a nice $9.00. Incidentally, the dealer will probably give you two red chips (a red chip is $5) and take away your dollar.

Of course, with double-odds you would have bet $10 as odds and been paid $15 if the 5 or 9 repeated. Just be sure the correct payoff never includes a fraction of a dollar. And to do that, you have to know what the odds really are.

Look at the chart again. *Think 6 to 5 for 6&8, 3 to 2 for 5&9, and 2 to 1 for the end numbers 4&10.* After a while, you'll know these simple odds as well as you know your own name.

By the way, don't think that payoffs are a problem just with small wagers. A $25 line bet with $25 odds for the points 5 or 9 can't be paid correctly either. You may go to the next unit value which is $30 to insure a correct odds payoff. Odds-bets with 5 or 9 the point, must be divisible by two. Similarly, odds-bets for the points 6 and 8 must be divisible by five. Points 4 and 10 are no problem since they pay 2 to 1. And everything is divisible by one!

Most players unfortunately make these mistakes because they have no inkling what the odds are. If they win, they're happy. *They don't realize they've just been shorted!*

The Odds-Bet is Easiest at Double-Odds Table

Since the size of your odds-bet seems to be the most confusing issue with new players, let's stay with it for a moment.

The easiest way to make sure your odds-bet can be paid at correct odds, is to play only at a double-odds table, with a red chip ($5) minimum pass-line wager, or any multiple of the red chip . . . two, three, four red chips and so on.

Of course, it also works for a green chip or black chip.

Green chips are $25 and black chips are $100, but that's a little steep to start with.

Assuming you begin play with red chips as I do, any odds-bet you make will be double any multiple of $5, and *divisible by both two and five*. It works. Take my word for it.

Incidentally, the casino term for the amount of your pass-line bet is called a "flat" wager. At the double-odds table, simply bet double the amount of your flat wager. It's that simple. You've made the right bet. You've reduced the casino advantage as low as you can. And you know your bet can be paid correctly if you play as most players do, with red chips.

It's a good rule to remember, and a safe betting amount to begin with. Red chips aren't "chopped liver." You can easily work your way up to a total wager of $90 in red chips, $30/$60, accumulate a few "greenies" in your payoffs, and feasibly win over a thousand in just a few rolls.

By the way, never be intimidated by the player next to you who's betting thousands at a crack. There's absolutely nothing wrong with red chips! Pay attention to your own bets, and be content with your "red" action.

Later on, we'll learn how to properly, and safely, press-up your bets as the opportunity arises, but only when you're ahead and winning!

Make the Most of Your Odds-Bets!

There's only one drawback to what we've just covered, and that's the fact that most casinos only offer *single-odds*. Fortunately, more and more casinos are changing over to double-odds, but what can we do to increase our odds-bet at the *single-odds table*, if that's the only table we can find? Remember that your odds-bet at a single-odds table is usually limited to the amount of your flat wager on the pass-line.

Actually, there are two ways to increase your odds-bet if

you're stuck at a single-odds table. And we've already discussed one of them earlier. If you recall, the casino will allow you to increase the odds-bet by a minimum amount to insure that your bet can be paid correctly.

In addition, the casino will also allow you to increase the size of your odds-bet to insure that payoffs will always be in chip values that are the *same or larger* than the value of chips you have wagered on the pass-line.

Here's an example. Suppose your pass-line bet is $30. If you made an odds-bet of $30 and won on a point of 6 or 8, you would be paid $36. Somewhere in there is a silver dollar. If you won on $40, your payoff is $48. A payoff of red, green, and silver dollars.

As a courtesy to the players (that's the casino's reason), they allow the pass-line wager of $30 to $45 to take an odds wager of *$50*. That's the next multiple of $5 chips that will yield a payoff that can be made *without* silver dollars.
Most casinos now use casino-issued silver dollars instead of $1 chips—too expensive to manufacture. The fake silver dollars are usually good in other casinos unlike chips, with the theory they're worth at least a dollar in metal. But don't try to use them back home. The MGM lion doesn't go over as well as Eisenhower at your friendly bank.

To push the point home about making this bet, here's one more example. Say your pass-line bet is four green chips ($100). If the point is 6 or 8, the casino will allow five green chips as the odds-bet. That makes the payoff easy. *Six* green chips to the *five* green chips wagered. No red, all green. Got it?

The Three-Unit Wager

When I play at a single-odds table, I make it a rule to always bet three chips on the pass-line. Here's why.

The casino will allow an odds-bet of five chips for the points 6 and 8, four chips for the points 5 and 9, and a flat wager of three chips for the points 4 and 10. That's especially nice because my winning payoff will always be *nine chips*. If the payoff is ever less than nine chips, the dealer mis-paid me and I won't pick them up until he sees the discrepency. Dealers do on rare occasion make a mistake. But not very often. Here's the "three-unit" bet rule to remember:

POINT	PASS-LINE	ODDS-BET	PAYOFF
6 & 8	3 chips	5 chips	9 chips
5 & 9	3 chips	4 chips	9 chips
4 & 10	3 chips	3 chips	9 chips

The bet is allowed, as we said before, as a courtesy to the player so that all winning payoffs are in chip values of your wager (or more, not less). Regardless, it's a way to increase your odds bet, especially when 6 or 8 is the point. Three red chips, three green chips, or three black chips . . . always try to make the three-unit wager at the single-odds tables.

THE COME-BET

The come-bet is best described as a "delayed" pass-line wager. And there's no question where to place it. The largest block of the table is assigned for a come-bet. The area has the name "COME" boldly displayed.

If you make a come-bet by placing a chip in that area *near your position at the table*, it's the same as a pass-line bet except that you're making the bet *while the shooter is trying to repeat a point-number*. That's the only time you can make a come-bet, otherwise the bet would obviously be placed on the pass-line since the bet is exactly the same.

Let's say the shooter's number to win on the pass-line has been established as 6. If you wish to have another bet working in addition to the pass-line, simply make a come-bet as I've described. If the next roll is a 9, you'll be looking for another 6 or 9 (before a 7) to win either bet. It can be said that you have two numbers "working" . . . 6 "on the line" and 9 "coming."

Had the next roll been a craps, you would have lost the come-bet. A 7 or 11 would have won outright, but remember, the 7 would have wiped out the pass-line. Mixed emotions!

When a 7 or 11 is rolled on a come-bet, the dealer immediately places the payoff directly beside your bet. It's your responsibility to *immediately* pick up the chips, otherwise the bet "works" on the next roll as another come-bet. On the other hand, if a craps is thrown, the dealer simply picks up your chip, and it's up to you to make another bet.

The Point-Box

Assuming the roll is a point-number, your come-bet does not remain in the come area. The dealer will reposition your bet in the numbered boxes for the point-numbers in a spot that's directly referenced to your location at the table.

If you're standing at the corner of the table, the come-bet will be moved to the corner of the point-box. That's how the dealer (and you) can keep track of your bets and distinguish them from other come-bets in the same point-box made by other players.

You'll want to make an odds-bet along with your come-bet when it goes to a point-box, for the same reason you must make the odds-bet behind your pass-line wagers when a point is established. Remember, it lowers the casino advantage considerably!

How to Make an Odds-Bet on the Come

To make an odds-bet in the come area, simply position the bet near the original come-bet and announce to the dealer loudly and clearly, "Odds on my come-bet." Do not place the odds chips on top of your come-bet, for obvious reasons. You recall, I hope, that the odds-bet is paid at correct odds whereby the come-bet (flat wager) is paid only at even money. You *must* keep the chips separate.

When the come-bet and odds-bet are repositioned in the point-box, the dealer places the odds wager on top of the come-bet, but *slightly offset* to distinguish the two different bets. Always watch the dealer to be sure he understood you and in fact, has your bets positioned correctly, and in the proper location.

When the shooter repeats a come-bet point-number for you, the dealer will immediately return your come-bet and odds-bet to the come area where you originally placed them.

Next, he'll place your winning chips directly beside the bet, for you to pick up. Again, if you don't pick up all the chips, they work on the next roll as another come-bet. Be careful!

Incidentally, when you make a come-bet and odds-bet, always be sure to position the bets in the come area *near the perimeter and in direct line with where you're standing*. Don't throw your chips or place them just anywhere in the come area.

Your bet may later be confused with another come-bet placed by another player. It's your responsibility to keep track of your own chips. There's always some jerk at the table who thinks *your* chips are *his* chips.

Why Make Come-Bets?

The best reason I can give you for making come-bets is to gang-up on the table when a shooter is repeating a lot of point-numbers that would otherwise be useless to you. Don't let all those beautiful point-numbers go to waste! That's your cue to make lots and lots of come-bets.

I've seen many instances when a shooter rolled the dice for more than a half-hour before he finally sevened-out. How nice!

Off and On

You can make as many come-bets as you want to. And when the shooter is throwing numbers, and numbers, and numbers . . . enjoy yourself! Frequently, you might have all five remaining point-numbers covered with come-bets. Quite often, the shooter will roll a point-number that you already have covered with a come-bet.

When this happens, the action is termed "OFF AND ON," meaning the dealer will simply pay your "net" winnings as if the chips moved about on the table as they normally would. Unnecessary actions.

The net result, if you stop and think about it, is that you win the come-bet with odds in the point-box, so that's what the dealer will pay you, directly beside your last come-bet. Pick it up and leave the last come-bet to work again for you. Your original come-bet with odds (on which you were actually paid) will also stay where it is in the point-box, waiting for another *off and on* payoff.

Off On the Come

The player may remove his odds-bet wagers any time, or simply call the bets "off" whenever he likes, on a whim or whatever. Although there's no particularly good reason for doing it.

Of course, the player can't remove a pass-line or come-bet. Otherwise, the player would have a healthy advantage, as we told you earlier by just letting the bet work on the come-out (where the player has a big advantage) and then simply taking the bet down if a point-number is established (where the edge swings to the casino). Obviously, the casino won't go for that!

But, since the odds-bet is fair, no advantage either way, the casino will let you do as you please with it.

They do however, have a standing rule that all odds-bets are automatically *off* on the come-out unless the player says otherwise (that they're working). The theory is that most players don't want to lose the odds-bets in case a 7 is rolled on the come-out which would wipe out all the come-bets placed in the point-boxes. The 7 will in fact wipe out your come-bets, but with the odds called off, the dealer will return all your odds-bets to you. It's a standard house rule, so go with it.

ONLY THREE BETS TO REMEMBER

We've just learned the pass-line bet, odds-bet, and come-bet in a manner that may have seemed a bit lengthy to you, especially if you're an experienced player. Sure, I could have reviewed the bets in two or three paragraphs . . . just like the casinos do for you in their little gaming booklets you can get free for the asking.

Purposely, I repeated important aspects of making these bets to help you remember them. Purposely, I went through it slowly with you, using many examples, to make sure you know exactly what to do, and exactly why you're doing it.

This is not a crash course. If you want a succinct explanation of craps, get the free booklet from the casino. But don't look for the bets *not* to make, or any mention of casino percentages. Don't look for fine details as I've given you. You'll learn how to play and you'll learn how to lose. You get what you pay for.

We've spent a lot of time on three particular bets that you can make at a dice table because frankly, *there are no other bets that you really need to know about.* Sure there are lots of other bets to make. But none are as favorable to you as the three bets we've concentrated on. Technically, you should stop right now, review the previous pages, and go play.

I hesitate to tell you about all the other bets you can make at a craps table, for fear you *will* make them. You shouldn't! But to make this chapter complete, here's a brief rundown of all the other bets. Brief indeed, because there's no reason to concentrate on any of them. If you forget them, that's better yet. Here goes.

PLACE BETS

For the player who's too anxious to get his money on the table, the casino will allow a bettor to "place" any or all of the point-numbers without having to go through the rigamarole of waiting for them to come up as a come-bettor must do.

But for this "luxury," you have to pay a price. Certainly, the casino won't pay correct odds as they do on your odds-bet. No way! Here's a schedule of how the casino pays place bets. Note the casino advantages compared to .63% on the pass-line and come.

PLACE NUMBER	ODDS PAYOFF	SHOULD BE	CASINO ADVANTAGE
6-8	7 to 6	6 to 5	1.52%
5-9	7 to 5	3 to 2	4%
4-10	9 to 5	2 to 1	6.67%

Granted, placing the 6 or 8 is not that bad, 1.52% to the house. Occasionally, I'll catch myself placing a 6 or 8 if the number's not covered with a come-bet. Still the casino edge is *two and half times greater* than a pass-line or come-bet with double-odds. It shouldn't be recommended.

In the event you *do* place a 6 or 8, be sure to make your

wager in multiples of six dollars, or six chips, because the payoff is 7 to every 6 you've wagered. For instance, if you bet $30 on the 6, the payoff is $35.

Certainly you can see why placing the 5 or 9 is a poor wager. Indeed, placing the 4 or 10 is totally ludicrous. If you're dead-set on getting immediate action on those numbers, at least "buy" the 4 or 10. That's the next bet to talk about.

THE BUY BET

For some reason, the casino will give you an option on placing the point-numbers. You can either place them as we've discussed, or you can "buy" them.

If you buy the number, the casino will pay you the correct odds, just like on the odds-bet. But they charge you a 5% commission to do this.

Since the casino edge on the points 5, 9, 6, and 8 is less than 5%, it would be stupid to buy these numbers. But on the points 4 and 10, 5% is obviously lower than 6.67% (the place bet percentage) so it does pay to buy the 4 or 10 instead of placing it.

So, if in your "expert opinion," a whole bunch of 4's and 10's are about to be rolled, go ahead and buy 'em. For every green chip you wager, the dealer will give you two.

I mention the green chip because 5% of $25 is $1.25, but the casino will settle for $1 even. Don't make the buy bet for less than $20 however, because the minimum commission is $1 (the smallest chip at most tables).

Technically, the casino advantage is a little less than 5%, but it's close enough.

PROP BETS

Our Chapter on craps cannot be finished without a discussion of "prop" bets, but believe me, *you will be finished* if you make them!

Prop is short for "proposition," and that's the name of all these neat little bets you can make in the center layout of the table. The bets are handled by a guy with a stick (cleverly called a stickman) who stands on the player-side of the table at the center.

Most players literally throw the chips to the stickman to be placed. Technically, you're suppose to put the chips in the come area and tell the dealer the bet you want to make. The dealer will then give the chips to the stickman for you.

But the dealers don't want to screw with these chips. So go ahead and throw the chips to the stickman like everyone else does.

It's appropriate to "throw" the chips because basically, you're throwing them away!

Each prop bet represents a "teardrop" on the casino's chandeliers. Remember that!

The bets are either a one-roll decision or "hardway." If you make a bet on the "hard-six," you win if the number comes up 3-3, and lose if the 6 comes up any *other* way, or with a 7. The accompanying chart details all the prop bets and gives the casino advantages. The heading is appropriate.

DUMBEST BETS AT THE DICE TABLE

BET	PAYS	SHOULD PAY	CASINO ADVANTAGE
Any-7	4 to 1	5 to 1	16.67% (Wow!)
Any Craps	7 to 1	8 to 1	11.1%
11 (or 3)	15 to 1	17 to 1	11.1%
2 (or 12)	30 to 1	35 to 1	13.89%
Hard 6 (or 8)	9 to 1	10 to 1	9.1%
Hard 4 (or 10)	7 to 1	8 to 1	11.1%

On some table layouts, the prop payoffs will be "disguised" as *correct* payoffs such as 8 for 1 on the hard 4 or 10. Sounds like correct odds, right?

Wrong! "For" means you don't keep your bet. "To" does. 8 for 1 is the same as 7 to 1. Don't be misled by the casino's cheap tactic.

DON'T PASS, DON'T COME, AND DON'T GET EXCITED

The areas of the table layout marked DON'T PASS and DON'T COME are for betting "with" the casino, and against all the other players, assuming they're not all making "don't" bets with you.

If the shooter doesn't make his point, you win, just like the casino. A craps roll on the come-out wins instead of loses, however the casino calls it a "push" on the craps-12. "Push" means no action . . . a standoff.

The casino advantage is about as small as the "right" side (betting the dice *do* pass) and the BAR-12 as the push is called, counts more than you think towards the casino's advantage.

The only problem with the "don't" bets is that you want a cold table to win. You're siding with the enemy.

I never play the "don't" side because it's too damn boring. No excitement. Which reminds me. Never yell and scream and wave your arms when you win because the shooter sevened-out. Other players may have lost thousands! You'll get "looks that could kill!" Be sure a security guard is handy if you plan on touting your win to the other players.

If you're the type who likes to antagonize other people, the "don't" bets were designed just for you.

CHAPTER 4

EXPECTANCY OF AN EVENT

The heading of this chapter may sound like something you'll want to skip over. In plain fact, you should read and review this section until you fully understand why dice come up as they do, and cards fall as they may. As a basis for discussion, I'm going to tell you a little story. It's a good set-up for the pages that follow.

Every morning starts the same for me when I'm on a gambling binge. I get up early (jet-lag), and hit the gift shop for a newspaper to read during breakfast.

On this particular morning it was *very* early, and the casino in the Dunes Hotel was nearly empty. One crap table was going with just a few players. It so happened to be the table near the casino cage, on the way to the gift shop.

I had no intention of playing. My schedule didn't call for gambling at six in the morning. Yet I was wide-awake and precariously anxious. Know the feeling? Besides, jet-lag made it seem like mid-morning; It wasn't *really* 6:00 a.m. And I wasn't really that hungry. Are you getting the picture?

I slapped my hand everytime I reached for my wallet. Finally, I decided to just *watch* the action for a few minutes.

Here's what happened. A shooter would either throw a craps or a number on the come-out roll. Another roll or two, then zap! He sevened-out . . . line away. I'm telling you it went on and on that way. God, was it cold! I felt sorry for the players. It was a massacre! Anyone who really wanted to play that morning had little chance. Remember, it was the only table open at that time of the morning.

Sure, a *don't* bettor could have cleaned up. But as I've stated earlier, I don't play that side. A cold table is too depressing.

So, I thanked my lucky stars that I *didn't* play, and proceeded to the coffee shop as I had originally intended. But that cold crap table stuck in my mind all day.

During the day, I played a little golf, relaxed, had a brief meeting with a client, and hit the sports books to get some lines. By evening, I was ready to hit the casino.

I have a habit of thoroughly "casing" a casino before I pick a table. Sometimes I feel like I've walked a mile before I sense any opportunity. The only table that looked good, strangely enough, was the same damn table that was frightfully cold that same morning. No way would I play it!

I drifted over to the blackjack tables and eventually found a nice spot. Within a few minutes I was up $400, winning two out of three hands. During my play, I couldn't help but hear the occasional cheers coming from the dice table . . . that *same* table. I tried to tune it out, play my cards, and concentrate on the count. I was winning, right? Why change?

The cheering turned to yelling and screaming. It drove me crazy. I scooped up my chips and hurried to the scene. There was a spot I could squeeze into so I threw out a $25 come bet. The shooter's number was 10. I noticed he had a very large line-bet, $500 with $1,000 odds (the Dunes allows double-odds).

The other players had large line-bets as well and lots of place-numbers covered. My come-bet went to the 9. I tossed the double-odds to the dealer, and before he could place it, the shooter threw another 9! I made another come-bet and covered the 6 and 8 for $60 each.

I can't tell you the feeling that came over me. It was like some damn fairy touched me with her wand. Premonition? It was more than that. I would have bet the proverbial "farm" if I owned one. I knew, positively, that this guy *was going to make his 10!*

You know my rule about starting with large bets; You don't do it! But if you ever get the feeling, like I got the feeling, you can toss the rule aside and hit 'em with all the guts you can muster.

I bought the 10 for $300 (my winnings from the blackjack table). Remember, I got to the table late and didn't have a line-bet*. The 6's and 8's were paying off so I pressed up the buy bet on 10 to over $500. I threw out a $25 hard 10 (I can count on my fingers the number of times I've made a hardway bet). What the hell was coming over me?

All of a sudden, the table jumped two feet! And what a

---

*Although I got to the table after the shooter established his point, I could have simply made a line-bet late. The casino doesn't mind, because here's where they have the edge. The come-out roll favors the shooter. However, it was wiser to simply buy the 10. Here's why.

You would put $300 on the line as $100 with $200 odds (double-odds). If the line wins, my profit is $500, even money on the line, and 2 to 1 on the odds portion.

If I buy the 10 for $300, I give the dealer $15 representing 5% commission, but I win $600 if it hits. Less the $15, gives me a profit of $585, obviously better than the line-bet, even with double-odds. Remember, when you buy a number, such as the 10, the casino will pay you correct odds. In this case, 2 to 1.

commotion! He made his 10! When the dealer gave me eight more green chips I didn't expect, I asked what they were for. He said, "It's your hardway, sir! He made it hard!"

As it turned out, I just caught the tail-end of a damn good shoot. But I left the table with over $5,000 . . . a table that couldn't put two passes together fifteen hours earlier.

What was different? It wasn't the dice. They're all the same. In fact, casino dice are manufactured within a tolerance of one ten-thousandth of an inch! Casinos are *very* concerned about the strict consistency of the cubes.

In stark truth, there was no difference at all! You must understand that the chances of that guy making a pass in the evening were absolutely the same as in the morning at that same table, or at any table for that matter.

Regardless of when you make the bet, where you make the bet, even if you're wearing your "lucky shirt," the odds of making a 10 before you make a 7 are exactly, precisely, 2 to 1 against it. Nothing can change that probability. Nothing!

DICE DECISIONS ARE PURELY RANDOM

Let's confirm that the odds of making a 10 before you make a 7 are indeed 2 to 1 against it. 2 to 1 means that in three trials, twice you'll make a 7 first (and lose), and once you'll make the 10 first (and win). It's not an absolute. It's an absolute probability.

Each dice has six faces. Since two dice are tossed together, there are 36 possible combinations or ways (6×6). The 10 can be made three ways: 6-4, 4-6, and 5-5. The 7 can be made six ways: 6-1, 1-6, 5-2, 2-5, 4-3, and 3-4. So the odds of making a 7 vs the 10 is 6 to 3, reduced to 2 to 1. Simple, isn't it.

Now you see why a 7 comes up so often. There are six ways out of 36 to make it—the most ways of all the numbers.

Six ways out of 36 means the odds are 30 to 6, which reduces to 5 to 1. Every time you throw the dice, you have a one in six chance of making a 7.

An 11 has odds of 17 to 1. Out of 36 possible ways for the dice to come up, an 11 will appear twice, 6-5, and 5-6. That means that out of 36 ways, 34 will be a number other than 11. So the odds are 34 to 2, reduced to 17 to 1.

If you have difficulty believing the uncanny accuracy of probabilities, get a pair of dice at any drug store or at a gift shop in the hotel/casino, and throw the damn things 360 times.

Record how many times each number comes up. Compare your results to the probability chart in the previous chapter. Of course, you'll have to multiply the chart-numbers by 10, since it's based on 36 trials.

You'll quickly learn never to dispute odds and probabilities in a random game.

Suppose you threw the dice and 11 came up three times in a row! The odds of that happening are a staggering 4,913 to 1 ($17 \times 17 \times 17$ to 1). Now, what do you think the odds are that you'll throw *another* 11?

If you've already thrown three 11's in a row, the odds that you'll throw another 11 are the same as at any other time— 17 to 1! Surprised? Don't be.

The fact that you've already thrown three in a row, has no "influence" on the dice. The little cubes don't have brains to "remember" the previous rolls. Certainly you can appreciate that each roll is purely "random," and *independent* of any previous results.

Overdue Dice?

By the same token, there is no such thing as a number being "overdue." The dice aren't keeping track. If a shooter has thrown the dice twenty times without a 7 appearing, the dice are not "ready" for a 7 beyond their natural 1 in 6 probability.

Do you actually think there's a "force" at work, urging the dice to come up 7, because it's overdue? A provocation of mathematical "energy"? It's as ludicrous as it sounds. Yet, many players believe in it as the basis for their foolish bets.

The toss of dice will always produce a random event. Maybe a 7, maybe not. You know the odds. It's 5 to 1 each and every time you toss 'em.

Hit the Wall

I'm careful to use the term "random" when defining a probability. Why? Because some shooters have allegedly mastered the art of throwing dice to the extent that they can "manipulate" the outcome.

Casino bosses are on the alert for this type of player. The obvious countermeasure is to insure that the dice rebound against the back wall. The wall is lined with rubber, molded in a series of small pyramids to create a random "bounce."

If a shooter continually misses the back wall, the pit boss may announce "no roll" and rightfully so. If the shooter continues to provoke the bosses, they will promptly take away the dice and pass them to the next shooter.

Don't get cute and practice manipulating the dice. I believe in playing *with* house rules, not against them. I despise the player who tries to cheat the game. It's cause for unnecessary and annoying countermeasures, and an inconvenience to the honest player.

Remember, the pit bosses are there to protect the integrity of the game, for the house *and* for the players.

Hot and Cold

Let's get back to the story about the cold dice table at the Dunes. That same table that got mighty hot in the evening. If we apply logical reasoning that the dice are in fact producing purely random events, how can the terms "hot" and "cold" have any basis for consideration? It's a gross contradiction.

I wouldn't play at the cold table on that particular morning, yet hours later the same table was on fire, flashing lights and sirens that any player could easily recognize. I bet heavily as if the dice were no longer random.

Does it make sense? Not really. Does it make sense to shop around for a good table, as I've stressed throughout this book? According to probabilities that are purely random, it makes no sense at all.

You'll hear the terms "hot" and "cold" frequently and you'll probably use them frequently. The earmarks are endless. A hot table is noisy; a cold table is quiet. A cold table has few players; a hot table is jammed. And so on.

Logic Vs. Feelings

Here's the classic battle of logic vs. feelings. We know there's no sinister "control" over dice at a cold table to keep them cold and take all our money.

We know there's no sound reason for playing boldly at a hot table just because the table's hot.

This issue nags at all players. You know the logic irrefutably, *but you can't set aside your feelings*.

I'll continue to look for the best playing conditions whether it makes good sense or not. I fully believe in probabilities, but I also believe in streaks. Regardless of better judgment, I don't expect a long winning streak to emerge at an ice-cold table. If it does, I won't be there to see it.

There's always the answer that the table conditions—hot or cold, affect your playing habits, discipline, and strategies. You tend to play poorly at a cold table, and correctly at a hot table. It's a weak answer, but I've heard it and now you've heard it.

Powers of the Mind

The bottom line on this discussion is the strength of an instinct and the powers of the mind that no one will ever solve. I can't pick 20 out of 20 numbers on the Keno board because they "flash before my eyes," but I can be blessed from time to time with just a taste of something that I would otherwise have no earthly way of knowing.

I'm sure it happens to all of us. *I knew that guy was going to make his 10*. You figure it out.

Parapsychologists investigate psychic phenomena, extrasensory perception, and psychokinetics. The latter deals with moving physical objects through the power of persuasion; mind over matter. Sounds great at a dice table, right? Personally, I think it's way out on a limb.

But the rest of it, well, many noted psychiatrists respect it with the utmost conviction through countless unexplained, yet documented cases. And these guys are doctors of medicine—eight years of medical school and two years residence . . . certainly not fanatics.

I don't try to cultivate ESP powers. I'm not the least bit interested in pursuing it. I'm no different than anyone else who on rare occasion gets a strong vibe that's surprisingly accurate.

A feeling that I'm about to win or about to lose; that I'm making the right decision or I'm making a mistake. I suggest you don't discount it. On the contrary, back it up with all you can muster.

On the other hand, you know and I know that no person

can call the dice before a toss at will, through devine perception or whatever you want to call it. No one can ascertain the value of a dealer's hole card, or the next card out of a shoe, using extrasensory powers at their discretion.

If and when someone actually does perform such miracles, you'll read about it in all the papers . . . *the second most significant event in the history of the world*!

CHAPTER 5

THE CASINO ADVANTAGE

In chapter one, we told you that the casino always wins over the long term. Why? Because each game has a built-in house advantage (percentage) that simply won't budge. Casinos, like any other business, are there to make a profit.

At the dice table, some bets have a distinctly large casino advantage, while other bets provide a modest edge to the house. Obviously, we're only interested in making bets that give the casino a minimal edge.

In blackjack, the casino advantage with basic strategy is about ½%. But most players do not play an effective strategy and in fact play poorly, giving the casino an edge that may exceed 5%!

In Roulette, the house edge guarantees 5.26% to the casino, and the wheel guarantees the player a spinning headache. If you want to be bored silly, dizzy, and lose all your money, try Roulette. There are no systems, and no "wheel bias" to look for. The house churns out their 5.26% on every spin. Forget it.

And then there's Keno . . . an outrageously stupid game to play. The house advantage is an incredible 25% or more, depending on the wager. The big lure is a $50,000 win for picking 8 out of 8 numbers, but the odds are 230,114 to 1! A keno wager is the dumbest bet in the casino. Stay away from it!

THE CASINO "DROP" PERCENTAGE

This is a good spot to mention the "drop" percentage all casinos use to estimate their "gross winnings" at the tables. The drop is the money that goes through the slot on the table and into the metal holding bin.

When you go to a table and ask for chips, your money is inserted into the slot. That's the drop. Casinos figure to earn about 20% of the drop, each and every day.

Don't confuse the drop percentage with the house advantage. The house advantage represents a percentage of all bets that should go to the house, as their advantage in the game. The drop percentage is that part of the player's stake that all players part with.

It's more correctly a measure of the "amount" of play, with the house advantage working against the player.

Let's look at the pass-line bet at a dice table to better understand the difference. As you know, the house has an advantage of 1.41% on each and every bet. That means that on average, you'll lose $1.41 for every $100 you risk. But as you continually play your stake, and play back any winnings, the bets are compounded until you lose the average 20% drop. You may lose more or less (or win) but on average the casino can correctly figure to win 20% of all the money that goes in the metal box.

The Longer You Play, the More Likely You Will Lose

Logically, you should be able to play about $7,000 in wagers on the pass-line before you lose the $100. This could best be shown by making the wagers $1 at a time. With that many bets, you're giving the 1.41% advantage the greatest likelihood of proving itself.

With these two percentages blaring at you, it becomes obvious that *the longer you play, the more likely you will lose*. It should be clear that your best shot is with fewer wagers, increasing the chance that the percentages will deviate in your favor. Over a long term, the deviations will tend to balance, and the house advantage always wins out.

We've just proven that the "hit and run" artist is an astute player. He wins and he quits. If you're fortunate enough to find a deviation, it's your opportunity to act quickly and press your winnings. Then quit!

Never grind it out over a long term. By doing so, you're giving the percentages too great a chance of working against you.

How Greed Affects the Casino's Drop

It's interesting how "greed" again enters into our discussion. Greed plays a big role in the difference between the casino percentage (usually small), and the drop percentage (usually large).

And the best example, once again, is slots. Although there is no actual "drop," the gross winnings are enormous! The "drop" at the slot arcades are the little booths in the area that make change, and the many change-girls that roam the area to convert your money into rolls of coins.

The casino percentage for a slot machine is called a "hold," but it means the same. For example, the hold on a particular slot machine may be 3%, meaning that 3% of all the coins inserted, on average, are "held" for the house.

So, 3% may be the casino advantage, but the drop percentage may run as high as 50%, far greater than the 20% drop associated with table games.

Since the drop percentage measures the amount of money a player loses in relation to his original stake, it can readily be seen that many players apparently feed all or virtually all of their stake into the machines. And that's precisely what happens!

New video slots offer jackpots that can make the player an "instant millionaire." To that end, many players give it all they have, literally. Not satisfied with a small win, or concerned with their losses, they put it all in and walk away with nothing.

That's what makes the drop percentage so large in spite of the relatively low house advantage assigned to most slot machines.

Fortunately, at the dice tables and blackjack games, we can assume that the player at least walks away with something, since the drop is "only" about 20%. Blackjack and crap players apparently have enough smarts to keep some of their winnings, or at least quit before they've lost all of their stake.

Consider for a moment, how important the relationship between the casino advantage and the "drop" percentage is to the casino. If the casino knows the drop will be large, that in fact the player will give most of his stake to the game, then the casino advantage does not need to be very large. And in fact, some slots are set for a very low percentage.

They tease you with a few more measly payoffs to make sure the player keeps on pulling . . . hanging on for the big jackpot.

Theoretically, if a slot player pulls the arm thousands and thousands of times (and sometimes they do!) then it makes no difference how small the casino percentage really is. As you can see, making so many wagers allows the percentage to simply eat away at you. If you continually play, the house will eventually have all your money.

Even a microscopic edge of .000001% will get all the

money . . . eventually, if the player has no concept of quitting. Take your few small wins if you're lucky, be thankful, and cash 'em in!

The difference between a slot machine with a small percentage and another with a large percentage can only be measured by the time it takes for a player to lose all his money. With the lower percentage, the player obviously gets to play longer.

If it's "entertainment" you want, you might wrongfully consider it a good value. But the results are most always the same. You lose.

Appreciate the fact that no matter how small the casino advantage is, the longer you play, the more likely you will lose.

HOW TO COMPUTE THE CASINO'S ADVANTAGE

In the previous chapter, we talked about probabilities in detail. If the house does not pay you at the correct likelihood of that probability, then they have acquired a specific advantage.

You already know most of the casino percentages for craps, blackjack and other games, but how are they computed? It's easy and it's important that you understand how it works.

A 5% Game

Let's pretend the casino offered a new game whereby the player simply flips a coin, heads or tails, and makes only $1 bets. If the casino advantage was a mere 5%, not unlike Roulette and better than some unfavorable dice wagers, here's how you would be paid: If you lose the bet, you lose $1, even money. And if you win the bet, you receive *only 90 cents*. Doesn't sound so good, does it?

In fact, it doesn't sound fair! Of course it's not. Nothing's fair in a casino. Remember, they have to pay their bills and show a profit. Their profit is that 10 cents they "shorted" you.

When you compute the correct payoffs and percentages, you must consider all the trials necessary for all the possible outcomes. When flipping a coin, there are two possible outcomes, heads and tails, so you must consider two trials.

Accordingly, 10 cents represents 5% of your total wagers ($2) for all possible probabilities (2). The percentage is not 10% if based incorrectly on the $1 losing wager, a common misunderstanding. Remember, you must base the percentage on the total number of trials (wagers) necessary to include all the possible outcomes.

4 The Hardway

Here's an easy example. If you bet $1 on 4 the hardway (2-2), the casino will pay you $7 if you win. But the correct odds are 8 to 1, so they should pay you $8. You are $1 short! Now, how many trials do we consider? It's easy.

If the correct odds are 8 to 1, there must be a total of 9 trials for all the possible outcomes . . . 8 trials you lose, and 1 trial wins. So, dividing $1 by 9 gives us 11%, and that's a mighty big edge. But, you knew it was a bad bet anyhow, right?

Here's a good time to mention the difference between "to" and "for" in stating odds. On the craps layout, it says that a hardway 4 is paid at 8 "for" 1. Be careful, that means the same as 7 "to" 1 because you lose your bet instead of keeping it. Deceitful? Don't be misled. 10 for 1 is the same as 9 to 1, and so on.

Big 6 On the Corner

If you place a $5 wager on the Big 6 or 8 at the corners of the craps layout, you are paid even money, $5, if you win. But the correct odds on rolling a 6 before rolling a 7 are 6 to 5. You should receive $6 to your $5 bet. Again, you're $1 short. And we know there are 11 trials (6+5). $1 divided by 11 is 9%, another bad bet at the dice table.

Incidentally, when you divide 1 by 11, .090909 appears on the calculator. Remembering your grade school math, simply move the decimal two places to the right for percentage, and round off the number. Technically, the house advantage on the Big 6 and 8 is 9.09%.

Place Bet on 5 or 9

Here, it's a little different because the payoff is 7 to 5, and the correct odds are 3 to 2. We have to assume we're making a $10 bet to compute the casino advantage. We would receive $14 instead of $15 . . . a difference of $1.

But, since we bet $10 instead of the $2 that our correct odds expression calls for, we must multiply the total of both numbers in the correct odds expression (5) by the number of times we exceeded the $2 bet (5) to yield the right denominator. 1/25 is .04, confirming the 4% casino advantage on the 5 and 9 place bet.

Keno

Let's prove that Keno is a bad game. Reducing Keno to its simplest form, let's pretend to bet $1 and mark just one number. Since 20 numbers out of 80 are chosen, your odds of picking a winning number are 3 to 1. But if you win, you'll only net $2 (they give you $3 and keep your $1 bet).

Since you should be paid a total of $3, but receive only $2, you are $1 short. Since the odds are 3 to 1, that means we have a total of 4 trials (3+1). $1 divided by 4 is a big fat 25%. No doubt about it . . . it's a lousy game!

Roulette

If you study a Roulette wheel, you'll notice there are 36 numbers, 1 through 36, plus 0 and 00, for a total of 38 positions. If you bet $1 on any number and it hits, the casino will pay you $35, 35 to 1. But we said there are 38 positions, so the correct odds of winning should be 37 to 1. Since you are only paid $35 instead of the correct $37, you are $2 short. Divide $2 by 38, the number of trials, and you get .0526315, 5.26% house advantage.

I told you at the outset that I would not overwhelm you with complicated formulas. Here's how another author on casino games tells you to compute the advantage: Multiply the winning payoff times the number of winning trials divided by the total number of trials, then add the product of the losing wager times the number of losing trials divided by the total number of trials. Here's how it looks on paper:

$$35 \times \frac{1}{38} + (-1) \times \frac{37}{38} = \frac{35}{38} - \frac{37}{38} = -\frac{2}{38} = -.0526$$

Correctly, the product of the above quantities should be subtracted since the losing wager is a negative number (-1). Adding a negative number in this case is the same as subtracting, for simplicity sake.

Both methods yield the same results, the correct answer. But isn't my way a lot easier?

Another bet at Roulette pays 11 to 1 if you hit any one of three selected numbers. To prove that this bet is also 5.26% in favor of the house, it may at first appear more difficult because the correct odds of hitting any one of three numbers is 35 to 3 (38-3 to 3). It may appear to be easier to use the mathematician's more complex formula, but not really.

To find out what we should have been paid instead of $11 for a $1 bet, let's convert the 11 to 1 payoff to 33 to 3 (multiply both sides by 3) and compare to 35 to 3. Now it's a lot easier to use my method. If you should have been paid 35 to 3, but instead were only paid 33 to 3, you're short $2 (on a $3 bet). And $2 divided by the same number of trials, 38, is 5.26%.

The Michigan Lottery

Lastly, let's look at a game outside of the casino. The Michigan Lottery. We'll prove that casinos are not the only source of bad odds. If you wager $1 on any three-digit number from 000 to 999 and win, you're paid $500. Does it sound good? It's a terrible bet! Worse than Keno!

First, let's find the correct odds. It's obviously 999 to 1 (one winner out of a thousand numbers).

You are paid $500 "for" 1 which is, as you recall, $499 to 1. A huge difference of $500! Divided by the total number of trials (1,000), it proves to be a 50% game for the State of Michigan!

Casinos would just love to have a game like that, but by law, they're not allowed to run a lottery. Numbers games belong to the States and the underworld.

Of course, when you win a State-run lottery, you're immediately taxed. Efforts are underway in most states to make state lottery winnings non-taxable, to compete with the other guys.

CHAPTER 6

BLACKJACK, HOW TO PLAY

Before we begin, this chapter needs an important set-up.

Blackjack is indeed complex, much more so than craps. It's as complicated as you want to make it.

Most gaming experts who have authored other books, steadfastly believe that you must keep a running track of all cards that have been dealt, follow an ever-changing basic strategy, and then adjust your betting for that rare moment (about 5% of the time) when the odds have shifted in your favor. In a nutshell, that's the computer-proven, mathematical approach to beating the game.

In order to keep an accurate "count" of the dealt cards, you must be able to concentrate fully. The casino won't let you drag in a portable computer terminal. Even a pencil and pad of paper are a no-no. To use the popular "count" systems widely advertised today, you simply must have a good memory recall, and the stamina to stay with it.

If you can't keep the count as you're suppose to, and you

flat-out refuse to learn "basic strategy," then blackjack will end up about a 5% game for the house, or better! More than eight times worse for the player than our best bet at craps . . . the pass-line or come-bet with full double-odds.

I'm not trying to scare you away. I'm just giving it to you like it is. However, as you read my chapter, you'll learn easier ways to keep a count. We'll take most of the complexity out of it! But there will be some work to do, and practicing your "skill" will be essential.

DON'T LET COUNTING TAKE THE FUN OUT OF THE GAME

My accountant told me recently that he's tried counting the cards, but gave up because it took the fun out of playing. He counts numbers every day at work, why would he want to do the same thing on his "Vegas" weekend?

Working at a blackjack table is like going to the golf course to mow the fairways! Counting is a lot of work. That's right, work! For the guy who really takes blackjack seriously, it can generate big headaches, even ulcers . . . just like at the office! And it can develop into an obsession. Not good. Absolutely, no good!

This problem brings to mind a strong conviction I have about gambling. *Never will I gamble a dollar when it isn't fun anymore*! I gamble because I enjoy it. I would assume you feel the same way. I assign only a leisurely corner of my life to gambling, no different than the typical "weekend" player.

Incidentally, in my opening chapter, in no way was I chastising the "weekend" player for his leisurely, fun approach to gambling. There's nothing wrong with having fun in the casino. The problem comes when your fun is spoiled. Don't let anyone spoil it for you!

The issue here is obviously *can we have both*? Can we develop a skill and retain the fun element of gambling? Of course we can. Learning a skill doesn't have to be a trade-off for having fun, and enjoying your "work." I'm enjoying every minute writing this book. For many, it would be a tedious, burdensome chore. The vast majority of my readers should be able to develop a sharp skill, and enjoy themselves in the casino at the same time.

As you read on, always keep our goal in mind. *To become an exceptionally skilled player, a winner, and have fun at the same time.* Be assured, I'm one author who won't take that away from you.

THE BASIC GAME

Blackjack is played with a standard deck of 52 playing cards, in fact the same "Bee" brand that you can buy in any drug store, made by the U.S. Playing Card Co. Jokers are removed.

You and any other players at your table (up to 7) are playing against the casino, represented by a dealer who merely deals the cards, and has no other "interest" in the game. The dealer's actions are mandatory, based on strict game rules. Technically, the game could be dealt by a machine or a monkey, since no playing skill is required.

The only possible "skill" to worry about is cheating, but frankly, it happens very rarely, if ever, especially at the larger, well-known casinos. Twenty years ago, perhaps. But today, with the priceless value of a gaming license, and the casino's ability to generate substantial income honestly, cheating is an inconceivable enemy.

Cards are dealt from a shoe (a box containing more than one deck) or by hand to the player and the dealer, each getting two cards. One of the dealer's cards is face-up for everyone to see, while the other is face-down.

The simple object of the game is for the player to have a hand that totals "21" or is closer to 21 than the dealer's hand.

The "number" cards count as face-value, the "picture" cards count as 10, and the "ace" is counted as either 1 or 11, whichever is better to make or approach 21.

If the player is unhappy with his hand, he may ask for another card, or as many as he likes until he "stands" (is finished). If the player takes too many cards and exceeds 21, it's an automatic "bust," and the player immediately loses.

When all players are satisfied with their hands, the dealer turns over the card dealt face-down (hole-card) and stands only if the total is 17 or more. The dealer is required to draw cards until the hand totals at least 17. If the dealer "busts" in the process, all players who did not "bust" themselves are automatic and immediate winners.

If, however, the dealer does not bust and has a hand that totals between 17 and 21 (which it must, because the dealer draws to make at least 17, and more than 21 is a bust) the hand is compared to the player's to see which is closer to 21. Whichever is closer, wins. If both the player and the dealer have the same total, it's called a "push" (a tie) and there's no decision on the bet.

BLACKJACK PAYS 3 TO 2

All bets that win are paid at 1 to 1 odds, which if you recall from our previous chapter means "even money." If you bet $5, you win $5, and so on. However, if the player's first two cards are a 10-value card and an ace, it's called a "Blackjack" (wins outright) and is paid at 3 to 2 odds. You'll receive $15 to your $10 bet.

If the dealer receives a Blackjack on the first two cards, the player loses at even money (only the amount of their wager) unless the player also has a Blackjack, in which case it's a push.

INSURANCE

The only other exception to the even money wagers is called "Insurance." Here's how it works. If the dealer's up-card is an ace, the dealer will ask all the players if they wish to take insurance. To do that, you bet an additional amount up to one-half of your original wager, betting that the dealer does in fact have a 10-card underneath, in which case you win 2 to 1 for your side-bet. The dealer always "peeks" at the hole card if an ace is showing to determine if he has a Blackjack, before the players are given the option of taking more cards.

In most casinos, the dealer also checks the hole-card if a 10-value card is showing, again to determine if the dealer has a Blackjack.

Today however, many casinos no longer allow "peeking" at the hole card (unless an ace is showing) to discourage collusion between the dealer and a player, attempting to cheat the casino. It's possible a dealer could "signal" the hole-card value to a player and thereby give the player a tremendous advantage.

The bottom line on insurance is *don't do it*! It's a silly bet that only increases the house percentage.

HIT OR STAND MOTIONS

To recap, the most important option the player has is to either "hit" or "stand." Your way of indicating to the dealer that you wish to hit or stand depends on whether the cards are dealt face-up or face-down. Some casinos deal all the player's cards face-up, other casinos deal the player's first two cards face-down.

Cards Dealt Face-Up

At tables where the cards are dealt face-up, the player never needs to touch the cards, and shouldn't. To signal a hit, the player may do either of two motions.

I prefer to point at the cards, actually touching the table with my finger about two to three inches from the cards. This way, there's no question that I want another card. Unfortunately, some casinos frown on this action for whatever illogical reason.

The other motion is to simply bring your hand toward you in a scooping motion. But be sure you do this over the table, so the "eye in the sky" can see it to record. (The casino's video-tape cameras are there to protect both the casino and the player. Don't be intimidated by them. Every table is in fine focus).

If you don't want another card, I recommend that you simply put out your hand, towards the dealer, as if to indicate "stop." The casino recommends a horizontal motion as if you're wiping a piece of glass above the table.

However, it's been my experience that the latter motion can easily be confused with the opposite signal, especially if the player is particularly sloppy with his motions. Try my way.

Cards Dealt Face-Down

At tables where the cards are dealt face-down, you obviously must pick up the cards to read your hand. If you do not want another card, simply place both cards face-down on the table and slightly under your bet. In most casinos it's all right to simply place the cards within close proximity of your wager.

If you want a hit, keep the cards in your hand until it's your turn to play. Then, lightly "scrape" the card edges on the table, towards you.

The instant you see your cards, make your decision right away! Don't guess. Follow basic strategy exactly! There's no reason to ponder.

Incidentally, it makes no difference whether the cards are dealt face-down or face-up in blackjack. This ain't poker! But, it does make a significant difference to card-counting that we'll discuss later.

SPLITTING

Another important option for the player is to "split" identical cards in your original hand, such as a pair of 8's. When this option is available, the player does not just automatically do it! The decision to split or not to split your pair depends on whether or not it will be an advantage to you.

When we get to our "basic strategy" later in this chapter, we'll detail each possible pair combination in comparison to the dealers up-card, and make the decisions for you.

For now, however, let's prematurely make two important rules abundantly clear: *Never, never, never split 10-value cards, such as two face-cards, and never split 5's. Always split aces and 8's!* If you're an inexperienced player, see if you can quickly understand the solid reasoning behind these two important rules.

When you wish to split your cards at a face-down table, simply position your cards face-up and behind your bet (to the dealer's side). Then, make another wager of the same size and place it directly *beside* (not on top of) your original bet. At a face-up table, you only need to make a new bet inside the betting circle to indicate the split, since your cards are already in position.

The dealer will know that you are splitting the pair, and will give you two more cards, one to each card you split, in effect establishing two new hands that are working for you.

If you receive another identical card, you may split again, and you'll have three hands in play. There is no limitation.

Splitting Aces

However, all casinos do not allow the re-splitting of aces. To make matters worse, after the dealer has given one card to each of the split aces, the hands stand. The casino will not afford you the option of hitting. Regardless, splitting aces is still a strong player advantage. Always do it.

DOUBLE DOWN

Here's an option that figures significantly in the player's ability to adjust the percentages. You may "double down" on your first two cards by making an additional bet up to the amount of your original wager and receive *only one card* from the dealer. One hit.

Obviously, the time to double your bet is when you have a hand-total of 10 or 11 and the dealer's up-card is 6 or less. That's the ideal situation. Another 10-value card will give you a 20 or 21. Even an 8 or 9 will give you a pat hand (17 or better). That's the reason we told you earlier never to split 5's. The two 5-value cards give you a hand-total of 10, and that's usually a good time to double down.

We'll give you the complete basic strategy for doubling down, and all the other player options, later in this chapter. You'll know exactly when to do it, and when not to.

As I've mentioned before, the casino industry has been negligent in their efforts to standardize game rules. Perhaps it's an element of competition that shouldn't be standardized. Whatever, the rules do vary, and doubling down is a good example.

Some casinos limit double down to only 11. Others allow it only on 10 and 11. Still other casinos will allow double down on *any two cards,* and that's a big advantage to the player, as you'll learn later.

I've listed the major casinos in the final chapter along with a schedule of playing rules that were in effect September 1983. It should help you. Unfortunately, most casinos not only have different rules, they *change* their rules about as often as your gas bill goes up. So the best solution is to simply ask before you play.

SURRENDER

"Surrender" is an option that few players understand or readily use. Probably because most casinos, until recently, did not offer it or promote it. Now, as blackjack players become more sophisticated and discriminating, casinos are turning to it more and more.

Eventually, it's estimated that virtually all casinos will have to incorporate it, in order to stay competitive with the casino "across the street."

This is what it means to the player. If you don't like your first two cards, and that happens a lot, you can "surrender" the hand and lose only one-half of your bet. To enforce surrender, simply state "surrender" to the dealer, and throw in your cards. The dealer will remove half of your bet and you're out of the woods. It's that simple.

I refuse to play blackjack in any casino without surrender rules. I don't want to hit a 15 or 16 against the dealer's 10. The only time surrender is not allowed is when a dealer has a blackjack. So wait for the dealer to peek when an ace or 10-value card is up. If the dealer does not have a blackjack, you're allowed to surrender.

A SOFT HAND

Any hand that includes an ace has two values . . . a soft value and a hard value. If our hand is an ace-6, the soft value is 17, the hard value is 7.

Although it doesn't come up that often, there's a decision to make whether or not to hit a soft 17, 18, or 19. Usually, a soft 20 is good enough and the player stands. But it's important to remember that a soft 17 will not bust. A 10-value card will simply make the soft-17 hard. Depending on the dealer's up-card, we actually may want to double down on a soft 17, if the casino allows it. We'll give you the basic strategy for soft hands in the following pages.

Dealer May Hit Soft 17

Earlier in this chapter, I told you that the dealer is required to draw to 16 and stand on 17. That's the basic rule on the "strip" in Las Vegas but in Northern Nevada and "downtown" Vegas the rule is altered somewhat, requiring the dealer to hit a soft 17. It's a nasty ploy, and definitely a disadvantage to the player.

On the table layout in "strip" casinos, it clearly states, "the dealer must stand on *all* 17's." Much better!

If you are inexperienced, or not an active player, I recommend that you review the previous pages before we go on to basic strategy. Be sure you fully understand the basic game, and particularly the player options: hit, stand, split, double down, and surrender.

BASIC STRATEGY (PRE-GAME SHOW)

Before we look at the charts, let's apply some good old-fashioned "horse-sense" and see if we can understand the reasoning behind them. You'll be able to remember the strategies so much easier if you understand why they work!

Stiff and Pat Hands

First, let's identify the potential "bust" hands as "stiffs." And it's a great term for them. When the dealer gives you

a 12, 13, 14, 15, or 16, you got "stiffed!" If your hand is
15 or 16, you've got one of the two worst hands possible,
and especially tough if the dealer's up-card is a 7 or higher.

Don't screw it up anymore than it already is by *not* hitting
it, or *not* surrendering it if you can.

If your cards total 17, 18, 19, or 20, it's a "pat" hand. It's
decent. Although 17 and 18 may be good enough to stand
on, they certainly won't get all the "marbles" all the time.
19's, 20's, and Blackjack's are the real "goodies" you're looking for.

Player Draws First

Judging by what we now understand to be the object of
the game, and the basic game rules themselves, it would
appear that the biggest casino advantage is the fact that the
player has to draw *before* the dealer does.

That simple fact accounts for a hefty 7% advantage to the
house.* So many inexperienced players sensing that problem, elect to never hit a stiff for fear of busting. That dumb
little ploy is worth about 3% to the house. We can work
down the 7% advantage other ways, but not *that* way!

Good Cards and Bad Cards

Now, see if you can identify the "good" cards and the
"bad" cards for the player. It's important. Think about it.

---

*Since all casinos pay 3 to 2 for a Blackjack, this effectively lowers the 7%
house advantage to a little less than 5%.

Player options based on "basic strategy," including hitting, standing, doubling, and splitting for both hard and soft hands will lower the house percentage
to about ½%. This number cannot be determined precisely because of variations
in rules from one casino to another, and the frequent rule changes that occur.
In addition, a multiple-deck game will add at least ½% to the casino's edge,
regardless of the player's counting technique.

Mediocre strategy may give the casino another 2-3% advantage. A poor
strategy may increase the casino's edge to 5% or more!

It would seem obvious that all 10-cards are good, because they help give you 20's, and pair-up nicely with an ace for a Blackjack. Sure, 10-cards are good!

What about 2's, 3's, 4's, 5's, and 6's? They help to promote those lousy stiffs, right? And more importantly, they can improve a dealer's stiff hand without necessarily busting. 2's, 3's, 4's, 5's, and 6's are indeed, bad cards!

Although we're getting a little ahead of ourselves, the object of *counting* is to determine how many 10-value cards and how many 2's, 3's, 4's, 5's, and 6's are *left in the deck*, based on how many you've seen *come out of the deck*.

When the ratio of 10-cards to "little cards" is high, the player has an advantage. If there are too many little cards left in the deck, the dealer has a distinct advantage.

Basic Strategy Depends on the Dealer's Up-Card

As you read the charts, you'll notice that our strategy depends on *both* our hand total and the dealer's up-card.

Applying the same simple math we learned in our chapter on craps, we can compute that the dealer will have a pat hand (17 or higher) *with a 10-card up,* about 60% of the time.

CARDS TO MAKE PAT	AVAILABLE
7	4
8	4
9	4
10	15**
A	4
	31

**16 less the 10-card showing.

Since there are 52 cards in the deck, the odds of making a pat hand are obviously 21 to 31, or approximately 2 to 3. To refresh your memory, the number on the left of an odds expression represents the number of times the event *won't* happen, and the number on the right is the number of times it *will*. To determine a percentage, simply divide the number of times the event will happen by the total number of trials (the total of both numbers in the odds expression).

$$\frac{3}{5} = .60 = 60\%$$

The dealer will have a pat hand *with a 7-card showing* only 40% of the time. And that's significant to remember.

Multiple-deck games will affect our percentages and the strategies that follow, but only to a very limited degree. However, it can be concluded that multiple-deck games are indeed an advantage to the dealer, not to the player!

Why Insurance is a Bad Bet

This is a good time to learn why insurance is a bad bet, and determine the odds of drawing a 10-value card at the same time.

There are 16 10-cards and 36 non-10 cards in a standard deck. 36 to 16 can be reduced to 9 to 4. So, the odds of drawing a 10-card are 9 to 4, unless you're counting, and know the random ratio has been upset.

The casino only pays 2 to 1 for insurance instead of the correct odds of 9 to 4. The difference of 9 to 4 and 8 to 4

(2:1) is one unit, divided by 13 (9+4) is over 7%, the casino's advantage.**

Now we know that the insurance bet is indeed a bad bet, and we've also learned that *the odds of drawing a 10-card should be considered 9 to 4*. As a percentage, it's 31% (4÷13).

HIT OR STAND STRATEGY FOR STIFFS

PLAYER'S HARD HAND	DEALER'S UP-CARD									
	2	3	4	5	6	7	8	9	10	A
16										
15										
14	S	T	A	N	D		H	I	T	
13										
12	H	IT								

ALWAYS STAND ON 17 OR BETTER!

Our strategy for hitting or standing with stiffs is really quite simple as you can see.

Always hit a stiff when the dealer has a 7 or higher. Remember it as 7-UP, and you'll never forget it.

Always stand on a stiff when the dealer has a 6 or less showing, with the exception of 12. The dealer does not have a pat hand (with the exception of ace-6) so there is a good possibility the dealer will bust.

**Technically, the casino's advantage on insurance is a little less than 7% because the correct odds should be adjusted to 35 to 16, in consideration of the non-10 card (ace) showing and out of the deck.

Always stand on 17 or better. Never, even in your wildest dreams hit 17! Dealers must alert pit bosses in many casinos when a player hits 17 or better. See if you can guess why.

Always draw a card on 11 or less. You might actually double down or split depending on the card values, but at the very least, you'll always hit it.

Incidentally, the hit and stand rules apply not only to your original hand, *but to your hand at any time.* For example, if your original hand is 10-4 against the dealer's 10, you hit it. You receive a 2. Now you have 16. According to the chart, you must continue hitting (until you have 17 or better).

Sure, the odds are against you, but you had a losing hand in the first place. Over the long term, you'll reduce the casino's initial advantage we talked about by about 2½% with correct hitting and standing strategy. Reducing the percentages against you is the name of the game!

HARD DOUBLE DOWN STRATEGY

PLAYER'S HARD HAND	DEALER'S UP-CARD									
	2	3	4	5	6	7	8	9	10	A
11			D	O	U	B	L	E		
10				D	O	W	N			
9							H	I	T	

Notice that the player should *always double down on 11*, regardless of the dealer's up-card.

Doubling on 10 is restricted to a dealer's up-card of 9 or lower. If the dealer's up-card is 10 or an ace, it's obviously too risky.

Some experts differ on the rule for 9, ironically. Our position must be to *only double down on 9 if the dealer's upcard is 3, 4, 5, or 6.*

It's a mute point in many casinos (especially Northern Nevada) where doubling is limited to 10 or 11. Doubling after you have split is equally restricted in many casinos. Ask before you play to be sure you understand the rules in a particular casino. Always seek out the best playing conditions.

Proper strategy for hard double downs (and for soft doubling that we'll cover under "Soft Hand Strategy") further reduces the casino percentage by about 1½%. We're getting there!

COURTESY: DESERT INN, LAS VEGAS.

SPLITTING STRATEGY

PLAYER'S HAND	DEALER'S UP-CARD									
	2	3	4	5	6	7	8	9	10	A
A-A			S	P	L	I	T			
10-10			S	T	A	N	D			
9-9										
8-8			S	P	L	I	T			
7-7										
6-6								H	I	T
5-5		D	O	U	B	L	E			
4-4								H	I	T
3-3			S	P	L	I	T			
2-2										

Most computer-aided strategies for splitting pairs are randomly defined, with no symmetry to recognize. It's exceedingly difficult for the layman player to remember. In fact, most player-errors in basic strategy are made when splitting.

Accordingly, I've taken the liberty of simplifying our splitting strategy to make it much easier to remember, with only a minuscule trade-off in accuracy.

Since the overall advantage to the player for correct splitting is less than ½% (the smallest of all the player options) there's no reason to be alarmed. The simplification of an otherwise complex strategy is justifiably appropriate for this text.

Here's how to remember our special splitting strategy:

Always split aces and 8's. Never split 10's, 5's and 4's.

Treat 5-5 as 10 and follow our double down rule—double if the dealer shows 9 or less, otherwise just hit.

Split 9's when the dealer has 9 or less, split 7's when the dealer has 7 or less, and split 6's when the dealer has 6 or less. Remember that the dealer's up-card is always the same or less than the card you're splitting with 6's, 7's, and 9's.

Only split 3's and 2's when the dealer's up-card is 4, 5, 6, or 7. Otherwise just hit.

SOFT HAND STRATEGY

PLAYER'S SOFT HAND	DEALER'S UP-CARD									
	2	3	4	5	6	7	8	9	10	A
A-9 (20)			S	T	A	N	D			
A-8 (19)										
A-7 (18)				D						
A-6 (17)				O						
A-5 (16)	H			U						
A-4 (15)	I			B			H	I	T	
A-3 (14)	T			L						
A-2 (13)				E						

Once again, our "soft" strategy has been ever-so-slightly simplified to make it easier for you to remember.

Always stand on a soft 19 and 20. They represent good hands regardless of the dealer's up-card.

Always double down (if it's allowed) on a soft 13 through 18 when the dealer has a 4, 5, or 6 showing. Otherwise hit 13 through 17.

A soft 18 is the most difficult to remember because there are three options. *Always double down on a soft 18 when the dealer is showing a 4, 5, or 6 (just like the smaller soft hands) and hit it when the dealer is showing a 9, 10, or ace.*

With a 9 or higher up-card, the dealer may have a better hand, so it does pay to try to improve your soft 18. Remember, you can't bust any soft hand with a single hit. However, if you end up with a poor draw, such as a 5, you must hit it again (hard 13) and take your chances.

SURRENDER

The rules for surrender are so simple, we don't need a chart to show you.

PLAYER'S HAND	DEALER'S UP-CARD
15-16 (hard)	7-8-9-10-A

Many gaming experts disagree on surrendering a 15 or 16 to the dealer's 7 or 8 up-card. Most all agree to surrender on a 9, 10, or ace up.

This is *my* book, so I'm telling you *my way* to do it. I strongly recommend surrender of a 15 or 16 stiff (except 8-8) when the dealer has a 7 or higher up-card, *if you're playing in a casino where they allow it.* You should be.

And wouldn't you know it, the casinos can't agree on surrender rules either. Some allow you to surrender your hand only after the dealer has checked a 10 or ace up-card for Blackjack. A few other casinos, very few, will allow the surrender before the hole-card is checked. It's worth nearly 1% to you. So look for it. Don't hesitate to lose half of your bet with a bad hand. It beats losing it all!

BASIC STRATEGY (POST-GAME SHOW)

Now that we have presented a solid, basic strategy, it's important that you memorize the charts, so you'll know exactly what to do with every conceivable hand and dealer upcard.

Find a deck around the house and practice! Don't bet a dollar until you've mastered the strategy.

The Advantage of Basic Strategy

What advantage does the casino have against a player with good, basic strategy? I was hoping you wouldn't ask me that question! Every gaming expert in the world has tried to come up with a nifty number. But no one can pin-point it.

Even with today's advanced, high-speed, powerful computers, no one can give you a precise casino advantage because of the rule extremes that vary significantly from one casino to another.

Is the game one-deck or a multiple-shoe?

Does the dealer stand on all 17's or hit a soft 17?

Can I double down on any two cards, or is it limited to 10 or 11?

Can I double after I split?

Can I resplit aces?

Is surrender available?

Can I surrender before the dealer checks his hole-card?

And as I've mentioned before, even if you know the game rules in a particular casino, they may change tomorrow. Totally unstable!

The Player's Accuracy

Suppose we could find an exact percentage based on a certain set of rules, and we could if we wanted to. Now what?

Do you play a basic strategy absolutely perfect? I doubt it. Are you mediocre? Probably. If you're a poor player, you'll give back most of the casino's 5% advantage or more.

Do you see the point? No player is infallible. To what degree do we correctly apply basic strategy? It's a significant question in determining the casino's edge.

The Advantage is Based on Long-Term Decisions

Still another matter that you must consider when weighing the casino's percentage is the fact that it's built on long-term decisions. Nothing says the percentages can't vary 10% or more during the short term!

If you remember, variations are what we're looking for at the dice tables. We called them "deviations" in probability . . . an opportunity, remember? The same is true at the blackjack tables. There are incredible fluctuations that can occur, especially with a single-deck game.

Hopefully, all the big fluctuations will fall in your favor, but don't be so naive as to think you can't lose ten hands in a row. You can, and you will . . . sometime. There are no guarantees over the *short term*. You must understand this!

An arbitrary percentage of 1% (an acceptable number) only tells us that over a *very long period*, we will probably lose $1 for every $100 we bet. It would theoretically take 10,000 plays for the casino to take all our money, betting $1 a hand. So, you can see that 1%, although a very small number, will wipe you out, eventually. Don't be misled by little numbers!

Basic Strategy Makes the Game About Even

I like to consider the casino advantage of ½% based on average playing conditions for an average player using basic strategy. My number is about as useless as any other expert's number, because of all the reasons we've just cited.

Of course, if an "exceptional" player has found a casino with "exceptional" game rules, blackjack can be considered "even." With surrender, the player may actually have a slight edge.

I got a big kick out of a leading expert's number for the casino percentage. He made a big deal out of it as if the "media" should report on his findings!

Not to embarrass him, I'll change it a little but keep the same number of digits. That's the ridiculous part. He says blackjack with basic strategy is .347%!

There's no qualification as to the particular game rules, and why carry it out to three places? It's a totally useless, meaningless number, unless you plan on playing literally tens of thousands of hands under optimum playing conditions without a single error in strategy.

What we *can* determine from our analysis however, is that blackjack is about as safe to play as craps. I'm not saying it's safe, I'm saying it's about the same. Using basic strategy (with 95% accuracy) and under "decent" playing conditions, I rate both games a toss-up.

However, if a player goes one step further and masters a count strategy to identify the fluctuations while they're occuring, blackjack is indeed a better game. Knowing to increase your bet size when the opportunity is there, and laying back when the opportunity is gone, is the tremendous advantage to keeping track of the cards.

Keeping track of the *dice* is a waste of time. Previous rolls have no effect on future rolls. But at the blackjack table, previous cards *do indeed* have an effect on future cards.

We must learn a strong count strategy to have any *long-term* chance. Coupled with basic strategy, a powerful count strategy is essential to winning. On to the next chapter. Counting!

CHAPTER 7

COUNTING THE CARDS

Many players today presume that keeping track of the cards is a relatively new concept. Surprisingly, the first count strategy was developed over twenty years ago in 1963, by Dr. Edward O. Thorp, and widely publicized in his famous book, *Beat the Dealer*. Thorp based his revolutionary concept on work performed nearly ten years earlier by Roger Baldwin and a team of researchers.

Baldwin developed a basic strategy for player options, much as we know it today. Thorp devised a system for counting 10-value cards, working in conjunction with Julian H. Braun, a computer expert at IBM. Braum became active in blackjack analysis on his own, and made significant individual contributions.

The original work of these principal founders has seen little refinement over the years. A testimony to the accuracy of their work. Baldwin, Thorp, and Braun deserve the lion's share of the credit for pioneering count systems and basic strategy. Remember their names, for they are the "George Washingtons" of blackjack.

In more recent years, other leading mathematicians and computer experts have contributed to the "common cause" including such luminaries as Allan Wilson, Charles Einstein, Peter Griffin, Harvey Dubner, Richard Epstein, Lance Humble, Carl Cooper, and Lawrence Revere.

Today, there are literally hundreds of blackjack systems available, some at ridiculously high prices, but all based on the original work of this elite group.

THE BASIS OF COUNTING

We've already hinted to you what counting is and why it works. In essence, we know that little cards help the dealer, and larger cards help the player. Based on that critical aspect, it would logically follow that you must keep track of the little cards and the big cards as they appear, and ascertain the remaining cards in the deck by simple subtraction.

Thorp's original 10-count system was never seriously challenged for accuracy. Indeed, who would be dumb enough to challenge a computer! The problem however, arose immediately. It was too complicated for the layman player to use! Thorp recommended a computation of 10-cards and little cards in the form of a ratio. The computation had to be done in the player's head. No easy matter.

THE POINT-COUNT

Finally, a balanced system of counting was devised whereby a "minus" number is assigned to a large card, and a "plus" number assigned to a small card. Forgetting the ratios, the player would simply count the plus numbers and the minus numbers to determine the deck construction at any moment.

Wilson, Dubner, Thorp, and Braun contributed to this new technique. In fact, Thorp issued a revised edition of his book in 1966 to include a "Plus/Minus" count system.

Today, the systems that are plus and minus numbers are commonly called "point-count" systems and are generally regarded as the most powerful.

A Typical Point-Count System

Before we give you an example of a good point-count system, we have to learn the exact "worth" of the particular card numbers to the player.

CARD	RELATIVE VALUE TO PLAYER
10	+ .5
ACE	+ .5
5	− .6
4	− .5
6	− .45
3	− .45
2	− .4

Roughly, we can say that 7's, 8's, and 9's are somewhat incidental, and not worth tracking for the typical player.

Assigning a point-number to each of the seven cards listed above, requires some severe "rounding off." Here's an example:

PLUS (COUNT +1)					MINUS (COUNT −1)				
2	3	4	5	6	7	8	9	10	A
1	1	1	1	1	0	0	0	1	1

There are many variations on this theme. Some "experts" suggest different point-numbers for the card-values such as −2, −1, and 0. Surprisingly, some popular systems based on a point-count do *not* include the ace. If you evaluated all the systems, it would appear that many of them are different just for *the sake of being different*! Everyone has to have their own *different* system.

This particular point-count system goes under many names. It was widely publicized by Braun, Dubner, and Lawrence Revere. In 1972, Revere wrote a highly successful book, *Playing Blackjack as a Business*, concentrating on counting systems more so for the active player than the novice. He includes several interesting count systems and variations on basic strategy that the player must make as the count changes. Indeed, it's no cinch for the typical beginning player.

This system, and many like it, represent a balanced count because the numbers assigned to the smaller cards total the numbers assigned to the larger cards. Remember, there are four different 10-value cards, so the total number for the large cards is 20. There are five small cards to track, so the total number is again 20 (4×5).

Disadvantages of the Point-Count

The numerous authors of these systems recommend that you begin your count at "0" and simply start counting up or down as you see the relevant cards appear. The drawback to the point-count systems is a double-edge sword.

First, you must keep track of two different sets of numbers (little cards and big cards), and secondly, you must count up and down, forward and backward. That might be easy in a quiet studio, but in a *casino*?

I found that it helped matters a great deal to start at a positive number such as "10" instead of "0." That way, the count was most often a plus number. I rarely had to count "below" zero. And, I simply gauged my number "which way of 10," not whether the number was plus or minus.

I discovered that it also helped if I completely eliminated

the "plus" and "minus" prefix with each point-number. Instead of saying "plus one or minus one," I would automatically add or subtract the point . . . adding the little cards and subtracting the big ones.

Whenever my count hit "14," I would double my betting unit. If it ever reached "18," I would triple the bet accordingly. Likewise, if the count dropped below "5," I would simply lay off. No bets, until the count "righted" itself.

Still, I had to count forward and backward, and keep track of two different sets of numbers. My personal experience with point-count systems was a disaster. Perhaps I didn't have the concentration required, or the desire to "work" while I play.

I discovered that I was winning more money at the dice tables, so I gave blackjack the "cold shoulder." Besides, I didn't have to *count* the dice! All I had to do was make sensible bets and apply a little discipline. You could always find me at the crap tables.

THE "GOLLEHON IMPERIAL" COUNT

The weakness of any point-count system is in its complexity. *Can you appreciate that any system, no matter how powerful, is of no value whatsoever to a player who can't use it*! There had to be a better way to track the cards. I searched long and hard to find it.

Eventually I designed my own system that had nothing to do with "plus" numbers or "minus" numbers. It involved counting only in one direction (forward) and only one set of numbers . . . the little ones. So nice!

Here's how it works. Through empirical trials, I determined that the average number of cards in one hand, *including my hand and the dealer's hand together*, was about 5 cards. A computer will come up with 5.34. I found the number was 5.27 based on 500 hands. Close enough.

One thing the computer *didn't* have to tell me was the ratio of small cards (2-3-4-5-6) to the full deck. There are exactly 20 small cards that we're concerned with so the ratio is 2:5. That means that for every 5 cards dealt (to player and dealer combined) 2 cards should be small ones.

"Five" was a nice multiplier for us, since 5 was our number for average cards per hand, and 5 was the second number in our important ratio.

Simply keep track of the number of hands you play and divide it into the number of small cards (2-3-4-5-6) you have been counting!

If I've counted 10 small cards after 5 hands, I know the deck is running about average. No gain for me and no gain for the dealer. I'll keep my bets level. But, after 5 hands, if the count was 15, that divides as 3, not 2, and signals a larger bet, because more than the random number of small cards are out of the deck at that particular point in time.

Incidentally, the easy way to keep track of the number of hands you've played is with chips. For each hand, simply add one chip to your special stack. Keep the stack separate from the chips you're betting. At any time, simply glance at the stack and read the number. I recommend no more than 5 chips per stack. After 5 chips, start a new stack beside it.

Some other experts will certainly find fault with my system. I have no doubts. But I can tell you this. I've been playing it successfully over a long enough time to have 100% faith in it. I've won considerable money with only a handful of losing sessions. Plug *that* into your computer!

Play the Gollehon Imperial One-On-One

It's paramount that you find an empty table. You must play the dealer "head-on." Additional players will screw up our numbers. I've always preferred to play one-on-one, regardless. More action! And no distractions from other players.

It's really not hard to find an open table, unless you're

looking on a weekend. Remember, weekends are the worst time to gamble. Too many players. Your options are too limited.

With my "Imperial" system, I elect to play only in the early morning hours, between 7 a.m. and 10 a.m. for example. At that time, you can usually have your pick of the tables. Sometimes, there are more dealers in the casino than players!

And the pit bosses don't appear to be that sharp early in the morning. They probably figure all the card-counters and highrollers are in their rooms sleeping. What a great time to strike!

This is not to say that you can't find an empty table in mid-afternoon, late morning, or in the evening. Of course you can, especially on weekdays except Friday.

The time of year is also a factor to consider. I avoid June and July like the plague. On the other hand, December and January are excellent months to visit Nevada. You'll have little competition for the tables. The casinos are usually wide open, if you avoid the weekends.

Imperial Betting Strategy

Here's the betting strategy for the Gollehon Imperial Count, based on your "reading," which is the number you get by dividing the number of hands played into your small-card count.

YOUR READING	BET LEVEL
Less than 2	Table minimum
2	1 unit
3	2 units
More than 3	3 units
4	4 units

Remember that anytime the reading is "2," it's telling you the game is running about average . . . no fluctuations. In other words, if your count of small cards is about twice the number of hands, hold your betting level at one unit because there's no advantage either way.

To clarify, let's say your reading is less than 2. An example might be a small-card count of 3 after 6 hands. That's a very poor reading of ½ (3 divided by 6). After 6 hands, the count should be 12! In that situation, I would seriously consider jumping to another table, or at most, betting the table minimum.

Hopefully your reading may reach 3 as would be the case if you've counted 9 small cards in just 3 hands. That's the time to double your bet size.

On rare occasions, your reading may be as high as 4, and that's the time to go for the "jugular." Bet four times your unit bet, and enjoy the moment!

I recommend starting with a unit bet of $5 (preferably at a $2 minimum table). Eventually, you should be able to work your unit bet-size up to at least $25, if you're winning consistently. Then, your four-unit bet would be $100.

Gollehon Imperial Vs. Multiple-Decks

The Gollehon Imperial Count works fine for both one-deck and multiple-deck games because it's based on a ratio, not on the total number of cards.

However, the multiple-deck is a disadvantage to my system, as it is to others, for much of the same reasons. *The larger number of decks will smooth out fluctuations*. There is less likelihood of a large deviation, either way. And as you know by now, it's the large deviations (for the player) that we're looking for when counting cards.

Accordingly, I only recommend that you play the Imperial count at single-deck tables. Never play my system, or any system, with a six-deck shoe. You can expect only modest fluctuations if any, and worse yet, expect over 40 hands!

Although the shoe holds six decks, the dealer cuts off nearly two decks to prevent end-play. That's to stymie the one player in a million who can memorize every single card, and then compute exactly what's left at the end.

So, we're looking at about four decks to go through, and that's not attractive to my system. If you can't find a single-deck game, at least look for a four-deck shoe, usually cut to three decks (net) for play.

Some casinos still deal a two-deck game by hand (no shoe) and that's much better. You can expect about 16 to 18 hands and a greater probability of fluctuations. But remember, you must be the sole player. That's essential to the system.

Gollehon Imperial Accuracy and Advantage

Computer tests will show that the selected number of 5 cards per hand for the Gollehon Imperial Count will yield some distortions in the "reading" because the true average is 5.34. Picky, picky, picky.

I want to make it abundantly clear to my readers that any distortions that might occur will generally be in favor of the player, because the increase in cards per hand will usually occur from the small cards themselves!

Can you appreciate the fact that if a combined hand (player and dealer) totals 7, instead of 5, it's probably because of extra small cards. You can't keep drawing 10-value cards. More than two is a bust!

So, the reading may be distorted at times, but usually to the "good" side, encouraging the player to at least react at the right time, not at the wrong time. The error simply means that on occasion the advantage may be slightly less than your reading says it is. It's a picky point, but some computer wiz will have lots of fun with it.

Based on mathematical compilations, the Gollehon Imperial Count should swing the overall advantage *to the player* by more than 1%! A significant accomplishment.

Detailed records of my original play further documented the 1% advantage at one-deck and two-deck games. Combined with basic strategy, it's a powerful tool!

Incidentally, you may have to alter basic strategy somewhat based on your Imperial reading. That's another advantage counting gives to the player.

For example, if you know the remaining deck is "10-rich," it would be wise not to hit stiffs, since a bust is more likely. Similarly, if you know there is an excess of small cards remaining, double downs should be avoided.

More About the Imperial Count

I indicated earlier that card-counters strongly prefer a cards-up game. Obviously, it's a lot easier to read the other player's cards when they're up!

But with the Imperial count, *it makes no difference whether the cards are dealt up or down,* because you are the *only* player! If another player decides to sit down with you, simply play out your hand and walk away. No problem.

The casino won't reserve the entire table for you unless you're betting a grand at a "pop." Just a bit steep for the average player.

Be sure you have the discipline to seek out the one-deck and two-deck games. And the discipline to leave the table when someone joins you.

Unfortunately, surrender is rarely offered at one or two-deck games. And you know how important surrender is, right? I was just about to tell you the name of the casino in Vegas that does offer surrender with a one-deck game, but they just changed the rules. Doesn't surprise me!

Our chart of casino rules at the end of the book, will be

assembled after the full text has been written. So, look it over closely. Just in case you find the combination of one or two decks *and* surrender, don't expect it to last forever.

By the way, I've taught the Imperial count to many of my close friends, and called it "Gollehon Empirical" because many of the computations were done mathematically, not by computer. I used the computer between my ears! Everyone thought I said "Imperial," not "Empirical," so the wrong name has stuck. No difference. Just as long as you play it, and play it well!

THE MATHEMATICS OF BAD CARDS

Just in case you have doubts about the negative value we've assigned to little cards, here's a set of basic tables that should convince you.

The first table lists the five stiffs no player wants, and the card values that can create them.

The second table shows the same stiffs, but with the card values that can make them pat. Since the dealer *must* draw to 16, and the player merely has the option, any card that can make a stiff hand pat is a disadvantage to the player.

TABLE #1	STIFF	12	13	14	15	16
	CARD	2−10	3−10	4−10	5−10	6−10
	VALUES	3−9	4−9	5−9	6−9	7−9
	THAT	4−8	5−8	6−8	7−8	8−8
	CREATE	5−7	6−7	7−7		
	STIFFS	6−6				

TABLE #2	STIFF	12	13	14	15	16
	CARD	5=17	4=17	3=17	2=17	2=18
	VALUES	6=18	5=18	4=18	3=18	3=19
	THAT	7=19	6=19	5=19	4=19	4=20
	MAKE	8=20	7=20	6=20	5=20	5=21
	STIFFS	9=21	8=21	7=21	6=21	
	PAT					

CARD VALUES	2	3	4	5	6
TABLE #1	1	2	3	4	6
TABLE #2	2	3	4	5	4
Grand Total	3	5	7	9	10

According to our study, 5's and 6's will create more stiffs, and make stiffs pat more than the other small cards. The computer will show that the 5-value card is indeed the worst, because the computer can run literally millions and millions of trials, taking into account doubling down, splitting, and values in consideration of other hands.

Technically, a computer would have difficulty for example, with our pair of 6's making a stiff, because at times the pair would be split, and the stiff avoided . . . maybe.

The data we gave you earlier that "rated" the negative value of the small cards should not be challenged. Our tables are merely to show you the effect the small numbers can have, without filling the book with pages and pages of computer print-outs. The evidence is indisputable.

BEFORE YOU PLAY ...

We must raise one more "warning flag" before we can officially end this chapter.

Casinos are bombarded with expert counters day-in and day-out. The best minds in the world have challenged the very existence of the game. Yet, blackjack is still there, in fact more tables than ever before. And casinos continue to win.

We'll give you some staggering numbers in our last chapter about casinos specifically, so you'll be able to see the consistency of their ability to win. Casinos win money. Lots of it! All the expert counters in the world pose no grave threat to their income.

The actions on the part of the casino, in view of the widely publicized count systems, have been more or less superficial. There are fewer one-deck games, and more shoes on the table. Six decks, and even four decks make it difficult to keep a count and minimize fluctuations.

Pit bosses are on the watch for suspected counters and if they detect any danger, the dealers are told to "shuffle-up." Premature shuffling stops a counter cold!

In some casinos, it's not unusual to set betting limitations or prevent a player from jumping into a game when he wants to. He either plays or he doesn't play.

Sure, the casino has taken countermeasures. And you would too if it were *your* casino! But the bottom line is that the casinos still win. The countermeasures, for the most part, are an overreaction. The great majority of players lose, even those who are armed with the best strategies available. There are no guarantees.

Without the discipline we've talked about and plain common sense, strategies are completely useless. I've seen too many expert players simply forget the meaning of discipline. Don't you forget it! *Discipline is still the most important strategy of them all*!

CHAPTER 8

HOW TO BET, PLAY THEM TOUGH!

In Chapter 3, we talked briefly about betting strategies during a streak. Remember the rule: *Always bet with the streak, never against it.*

Our example was ten winning hands in a row at blackjack. Indeed it's a rare occasion, but it happens at least once or twice for me during a typical two or three day visit. Never let it slip by, and never jump out of it with reverse betting.

	BETTING SCHEDULE A (RED)	PERCENTAGE OF INCREASE	BETTING SCHEDULE B (GREEN)	
1.	$ 15		$ 75	
2.	25	60%	125	
3.	40		200	
4.	65		325	
5.	90		450	
6.	125	40%	625	
7.	175		875	
8.	250		1250	
9.	325		1625	
10.	425	30%	2000	(table limit)
11.	550		2000	
12.	700		2000	

BETTING A STREAK!

Betting Schedule A is for the small bettor beginning the session with a $15 opening bet. Schedule B is for the player who can afford a much greater initial risk. Regardless of your income, I don't recommend starting with large bets, but it's your money.

Let's use the same ten winning blackjack hands in a row as an example to follow. With the proper betting strategy, the 11th bet should be $550 for the small bettor. Betting $15 is easy. Betting $550 takes some guts for the average player with an average income.

Sure, you might lose it. But going into that bet, you're up $1,535. If you lose the 11th hand, you would say goodbye to the streak with 935 smackers! Not bad for about 15 minutes play, and putting only a modest stake in jeopardy.

Perhaps you're starting this streak well into a winning session, and you've been pressing your bets as you should do. The small bettor might actually follow the Schedule B format, because at the start of the streak, you will have had pressed up previous bets to the $75 level or more.

Using your winnings, instead of your hard earned money you came with, you're now in position to follow the high-roller's strategy and win it big! In fact, 10 winning hands in a row at the "B" schedule, yields a tidy $7,550! At the 10th level, you've reached the "table maximum" bet of $2,000!

By the way, "pressing" does not mean "doubling." Maybe on the golf course, but not in this book. Doubling is not reflected in either schedule to protect any win. Pressing means increasing the size of your previous bet by an amount I have assigned in the Schedules.

Other Betting Progressions

Incidentally, there are numerous other betting progressions that differ vastly from mine. Many I've studied are based on large presses as the streak continues.

I differ strongly with that theory based on the absolute probabilities of the streak at selected levels. Correctly, the increases should be large at the *beginning*, where the greater chance of a streak exists, and *reduced* significantly as the streak continues, since the very likelihood of the streak itself is continually diminishing.

Can you appreciate that it's much easier to put four or five winning hands together as opposed to nine or ten. Accordingly, the percentage of increase must be tailored to the streak's mathematical probabilities.

Don't Miss a Rare Opportunity

The emotional high of winning big on a streak is equal in intensity to the depression of *not* winning much at all because you watched it go by. It's a hollow feeling when you think about how much you *could have won*. Don't let it happen.

It brings a tear to my eye to see a little old lady betting a single red chip on each hand as she rides an incredible streak. And I've seen it happen too often. Instead of winning thousands, she wins a few dollars.

Sometimes the streaks are not as evident at dice as they are at blackjack. Recently at Caesar's Palace, I watched a shooter make 12 passes. For some reason, I jumped in late. Just not paying attention. At no time were any other players making sizable bets. We were all acting like "zombies."

When the shooter finally sevened-out, a floorman came over to me and just shook his head. "This table should have lost a hundred grand with a shoot like that," he said. He motioned around the plush casino and said, "That's how we pay for all of this."

Streaks of that magnitude are indeed rare, but they *will* happen and you must be prepared for it. Streaks are the only time I'll ever veer from the betting strategy for my Imperial count. Just because my count-reading might be poor, it certainly doesn't mean I've got a guaranteed loser!

If I'm riding a streak, I'll continue to press my bets regardless of the count-reading. Many authors will disagree with me on this notion. None-the-less, nothing, absolutely nothing, will keep me from pressing during a streak, unless of course, my wife walks up to the table and asks me, "How are you doing?"

Know When to Bet Down

So what do we do if we're into a streak, but it collapses before we could put at least seven or eight together. *That's when you bet down*! Don't under any circumstances, continue pressing. I'll generally reduce my bet by 50% or more. If I lose the next hand, I'll drop down to the beginning of the "A" Schedule. I might very well cash-out and count my winnings.

By doing this, you're following the classic rule of smart betting. *Press up the winnings, lay back on the losses*. Should losing hands prevail, I'll get a copy of Wall Street and lie by the pool. As I said before, I like to hit and run.

Don't wander around the casino. If you make the circuit enough times, you'll probably end up at the same table.

The $2 Bettor

According to many casinos large and small, the average beginning bet at a blackjack table is $5, a single red chip. It's an average based on all the tables from a $2 to $100 minimum.

Each table has its own minimum bet posted clearly, and usually color-coded.

Obviously, there's a large number of $2 bettors. And I think that's just fine and dandy. You won't get hurt, and you'll have plenty of fun.

So, begin with the $2 bet, and if you're winning regularly, press up to $3, then $5, $7, $10, and so on, in increments that make you feel comfortable. You might get to a $15 bet, and from there, cross your fingers and follow the Schedule A format above. Let's say you make it to the 4th level, but lose the 5th. Drop back to your silver dollars, count your winnings, and wait for another ride up.

THE GREEN CHIP BETTOR

At this stage, we've discussed all the essential rules of discipline, the fundamentals of blackjack, and how to play craps with sound, sensible betting. All in all, it might appear as if we need super-human talents or full-time devotion to function at the tables without error, remembering all the things to do and not to do.

Indeed, it's *not* the purpose of this book to turn you into a professional gambler. My singular concern is to teach you how to *play* as the professional does; armed with confidence, skill, and strategies to make the "professional" plays, and hopefully win more times than you lose.

For many players, some minor adjustment may be all it takes to seriously challenge the casino. For others, I recommend taking it one step at a time, certainly one *game* at a time. I suggest the beginning player limits his time at the tables. And after each brief session, review what happened, recall your actions, and determine in your own mind if you acted correctly.

Is there anyone who typifies the "perfect" player? Since this is my book and my typewriter, I suppose I could tell you I'm that guy, but in reality I make betting mistakes from time to time, and occasionally an error in discipline. Indeed, you will also. The question is how few mistakes will you make, and will you *learn* from them.

Recently at the Dunes in Las Vegas, I met a "New Yorker" while playing at a dice table. We became friends, and played together frequently. Watching him play was a sheer delight. He played the games (especially craps) as perfectly as anyone I've ever known. In fact, I learned a great deal from him. Unknowingly, he's contributed greatly to this book.

I imagine he still frequents Vegas occasionally, although with Atlantic City going strong, he probably plays there more routinely. Here's what he does.

First of all, he prefers a hotel that has double-odds on craps (and surrender rules for blackjack). Surprisingly, he wants a hotel with a sensible room rate. He refuses comps for much the same reasons I do.

I remember he told me that he stayed at Caesar's Palace and paid over a hundred dollars for an average room. Now, he said he stays at the Dunes for less than half that much, and gets a nicer room to boot. I'm telling you this so you can see how the guy puts a value on things.

With that in mind, can you appreciate how he handles his chips at the tables? Here's a player who earns in the low six figures, and he shops for a room rate. I don't know about you, but I'm impressed.

In the casino, he stalks the tables like a lion. He'll analyze and literally test a particular table *before* he sits down. He doesn't want to get ambushed! At craps, he starts with a single green chip ($25) on the pass line. He takes full double-odds, then waits.

If he's up a few chips, he'll make a second bet on the come. With the determination of a disciplined player, he'll stop with that bet, wait for a decision, then either go back to a single line-bet, or add a third come-bet to his well-planned attack. On numerous occasions, I watched him play with four come-bets working. Lots of action!

It's no secret that the pass-line bet (and come-bet) with double-odds is the best bet at the dice table. That's all he plays—line-bets with full double-odds, and a number of come-bets as a function of his win status.

Incidentally, he gave me some great advice that I want to pass along to you. If you ever get the urge to make a foolish "prop" bet such as a hardway, C&E, or hop-bet, simply put the chip *in your pocket* instead of tossing it out on the table. By the end of the evening, you'll be happy to discover those "extra" chips you would have otherwise thrown away.

At the blackjack tables, he begins with a single green chip. If he's ahead significantly at any point, he'll press the bet fully to two green chips ($50). From that point, he'll play another spot at the table if he continues to win, instead of pressing his original bet anymore. In most casinos, you are allowed to play multiple spots provided each bet is at least two times the table minimum. At best, he'll have four green chips in play.

He counts 4's, 5's, and 6's against face cards and aces, prefers a single or two-deck game, and uses surrender on 15's and 16's against a dealer's 7 or higher.

Contrary to my recommendation of pressing up each bet (30-60%) as you progressively win, he keeps his bets linear as a general rule, and simply adds to his *quantity* of bets as a form of pressing.

In further contrast, he begins play with a green chip ($25). That's definitely too much for the average player, more than I've suggested in this book, but certainly comfortable for him in view of his prosperity.

The exact amount of your opening wager is not that important, provided it's not excessively large, and remains constant.

Make a decision right now as to an opening bet that for *you* is safe and sensible. Then stay with it each time you begin play. Train yourself to automatically begin with that size bet each time you walk up to a new table. It's a very important aspect of your game.

In an earlier chapter on betting strategy, I recommended a beginning wager of $15 (three red chips) for the average player with an average income. That size wager at a dice table with double-odds should be placed as *$5 on the line, and $10 odds behind it.*

Another "character" trait of our "green chip" bettor is a cunning instinct to "quit winners!" He's a "hit and run" artist, like I am. The casinos hate it! When it comes time to cash-in, he usually has a few black chips ($100) to sweeten the win. Does he bet them? No way! He *accumulates* them, by asking the dealers for an occasional color change. It's his way of keeping track of the chips he *keeps*, and the chips he *plays*.

Most winning players will ask the dealer to "change color" before they leave the table so they have fewer chips to carry. What a pleasant thought! I hope you'll be asking the dealers to do this for you often!

In summary, my friend uses common sense and strict discipline . . . never varying from his rigid game-plan. He's professional and he's tough. Telling you about him is the best lesson I can give you.

Incidentally, if you play in Atlantic City, and see a distinguished, gray-haired, "banker-type" playing green chips exactly as I've detailed, say "hello" for me and tell him I owe him a royalty!

YOUR BETS SHOULD NOT REFLECT YOUR INCOME

Let's make an important distinction. *All rich players don't make big bets, and all big bets don't come from rich players.*

It's unfortunate indeed that so many players get in over their head. Compulsive, depressed, and near ruin. A player can be easily recognized making bets he simply can't afford. *Never make a wager you can't afford to lose.* Take the worm, but don't swallow the hook.

At the other end is the player who could buy the casino, having the time of his life with $2 bets.

At the MGM Grand in Las Vegas a few years ago, I played with a competitor in my business, but a good friend, who's easily worth millions. When he began to win a few dollars, I told him to press up. He appeared nervous and unsettled with the "big" bet out . . . all of $25! He went back to the red chips on the next shoot.

He wanted *only to win* and to *enjoy the time*. A loss might have upset him. A big win to him would have meant nothing. He makes thousands of dollars a week just managing his investments!

Can you be satisfied with a win of any amount, and do you know how to enjoy the moment? It's a rare quality.

Remember that winning any amount means you haven't lost. And losing, in any amount, often times is what you're really afraid of—the real underlying hurt. So often, it's not the amount you lost, it's the stigma of losing.

TIPPING

Since this is the chapter on betting, it's as good a place as any to discuss tipping. In Las Vegas, and all the other gambling centers, you tip the sky-cab, tip the porter, tip the cabby, tip the valet, tip the guy by the pool, tip the bellman, tip the maid, tip the guy in the men's room, tip the waitress, tip the maitre d', tip the guy who lost your clubs, and tip the guy who found them. And we can't forget the dealers.

Incidentally, I tip only when I win, and only at the end of a session. I rarely make a bet for a dealer. Not surprisingly, they prefer the tip, not the bet.

In any event, I tip in Las Vegas for the same reasons anywhere else. For good service! If the service is poor, I don't tip at all! Neither should you.

Tip only for polite, efficient, or helpful service, and tip appropriately. Don't short-change the guy who sincerely wanted to help you make the airport with time to spare.

CHAPTER 9

THE CASINO, A MIGHTY FORTRESS!

LAS VEGAS

Commercial airliners serving Las Vegas deliver nearly five million passengers a year to McCarren International Airport. More than that number *drive* to Las Vegas, especially from the richly populated areas of Southern California, bringing the total number of visitors to over 11.6 million each year.

Surveys indicate that many simply come for vacations; to see the fabulous shows; the glitter and excitement of a 24-hour city; and simply to enjoy the dry, hot, tanning climate.

Las Vegas is indeed a resort to vacation, rest, and relax. There are pools, tennis courts, golf courses, spas, and scenic tours to the mountains, the Grand Canyon, and to Hoover Dam. It's a vacationer's paradise!

But the fact is, *without gambling* Las Vegas would be just another ghost town in the desert. The great majority come to gamble. Make no mistake. And gamble they do!

THE LAS VEGAS "STRIP" AND "GLITTER GULCH" (DOWNTOWN).
COURTESY: THE LAS VEGAS NEWS BUREAU.

In 1982, Las Vegas casinos reported a gross gaming revenue of $1,751,421,394! Over 1.7 *billion* dollars! That number represents the "win" in all casinos before operating expenses. And it does *not* include other profitable hotel operations such as restaurants, shops, and the rooms themselves.

The Nevada Gaming Commission reported that all casinos in Nevada amassed a record 2.6 billion in gross gaming revenue, during 1982. Las Vegas alone contributed 67%! Las Vegas is indeed the crown jewel of the world's gambling meccas.

NORTHERN NEVADA

Reno and Lake Tahoe in Northern Nevada offer a break in the climate compared to Las Vegas, and have more outdoor recreation that surprisingly accounts in part for 77% of the visitors (according to the Reno Convention and Visitors Authority).

Reno sits peacefully at the edge of the Great Basin, and at the foothills of the majestic Sierra Mountains. Where Las Vegas has Palm trees, Reno has Pine trees, and more lakes, rivers, and hills to go with them.

Less than an hour away, and 6,200 feet up, is Lake Tahoe. A breath-taking retreat that words can't describe. There's boating, hunting, fishing, camping, and hiking in the summer, and a super ski area in the winter. Over twenty resorts offer downhill and cross-country, including the longest single run of over seven miles! Nothing can match the splendor of the High Sierras, and the 70 miles of Lake Tahoe shoreline.

But what about "indoor" recreation? Not everyone goes to Reno or Lake Tahoe for sailing or skiing. No Sir! Casinos abound! Nevada is Nevada, north or south. The chief difference between Las Vegas and Northern Nevada casinos is the size of the hotels.

Most hotels in Reno and Lake Tahoe offer less than 400

COURTESY: THE RENO CONVENTION AND VISITORS AUTHORITY.

rooms. The biggest exception however, is the MGM Grand with over 2,000 rooms! And, the largest casino in the world! It's as if someone "lifted" it out of Las Vegas and "plopped" it down in Reno.

Personally, I prefer the more relaxed "pace" and Western "charm" associated with Northern Nevada. Not surprisingly, I find that dealers and everyone who waits on you, seem to be more friendly.

With a population of just over 100,000, Reno is considerably smaller than Las Vegas. Where Las Vegas has over 50,000 hotel rooms, Reno has less than 9,000. No problem! That famous sign says it best. Reno's the "Biggest Little City in the World!"

On the south shore of Lake Tahoe, in a little town called Stateline, population 5,368, are five hotel/casinos. And the residents are proud of that number.

For many years, environmental groups have fought to preserve the Lake Tahoe region and prevent further growth of hotels and casinos up and down the lakeshore.

According to Bob Anderson, marketing director of the Lake Tahoe Visitors Bureau, ". . . future development would have far reaching negative effects on the air and water quality," and would "seriously jeopardize the unique beauty and experience of Lake Tahoe." Their efforts have apparently won out, because Anderson claims, ". . . no more (hotel/casinos) will ever be built in this area."

Anderson's secretary told me that occasionally someone calls her office and asks, "Are there any grocery stores up there?" Yes! Lake Tahoe has grocery stores, shopping malls, banks, *and* casinos! Five. Five today, and five tomorrow.

What they will *always* have is a crystal-clear lake.

ATLANTIC CITY

For over 45 years, Nevada held a monopoly on casino gambling in the United States. The only state where it was legal. Then, in 1976, voters in New Jersey legalized casino gambling to take effect in 1978, when the first casino, Resorts International, opened its doors.

It was a mad-house! Players by the thousands literally stood in long lines behind each chair at each table, waiting for their chance to play. What a novelty to be gambling in "Jersey," just like in Vegas!

Since then, nine casinos are thriving in Atlantic City and giving serious challenge to Las Vegas. In 1982, all nine casinos reported a gross win of $1,484,750,464! That's nearly 85% of Las Vegas gaming revenue for the same period. And we're comparing only nine casinos in Atlantic City to 61 in Las Vegas! Obviously, Atlantic City is *very* busy!

It's a surprise to many casino executives in Las Vegas who at first gave Atlantic City little chance of matching their numbers. "Atlantic City in January!"

True, Atlantic City doesn't have the nice year-around climate and magnificent scenery that Nevada has. You won't find the Mojave Desert or the Sierra Mountains out East!

They *do* have an ocean. But they also have January! January in Atlantic City is no time to lie by the pool! Unless it's inside. Inside where the tables are! As long as the tables are inside, who cares what's outside, right?

Now, Atlantic City is racing to become the "Vegas" of the East, if it hasn't already.

Atlantic City's Future Developments

The Atlantic City Casino Hotel Association reports that eight more casinos are scheduled for construction. Three present hotels: Caesars, Golden Nugget, and Resorts International plan to construct a second hotel within the next year or so.

In addition, the Camelot, Dunes, Harrah's, Hilton, and Penthouse have received building approval and have plans underway for pretentious hotel/casinos costing upwards of $300 million!

At present, Atlantic City has a total of 4,788 rooms, with each hotel averaging about 500. With the expansion plans I've just cited, that number could easily triple within the decade.

Comparing the number of rooms in Atlantic City to Las Vegas is no contest! Yet, the action at the tables is nearly a dead-heat. The reason, according to an Atlantic City casino spokesman, is that Las Vegas hotels ". . . book a lot of 'watchers.' " Obviously, Atlantic City hotels fill their rooms with gamblers!

The Atlantic City Casino Hotel Association projects that the gross gaming revenue for 1983 will meet or exceed that of Las Vegas!

Why? Mainly because Atlantic City is situated within one hour's driving distance of 25% of the total country's population! Over 55 million people!

That compares to Southern Nevada, in a desert, and within four hours driving distance for only 16 million potential players.

Besides, Nevada caters to gamblers *and* vacationers. In addition, Las Vegas draws many large conventions each year that fill up the 50,000 rooms in over 60 hotels. How many of these people do you suppose are highrollers? Like the guy in Atlantic City said, a lot of them just "watch" and lie out in the sun! Generally, when you go to Atlantic City, you go to gamble!

WHERE TO PLAY

If you live in Philadelphia, it makes good sense to play in Atlantic City, right? Why fly all the way to Vegas and pay the big airfare? In fact, that's the casino's theory about their markets.

Atlantic City figures to attract the East Coast, while Nevada continues to lure the West Coast players. People who live in the Midwest will elect to go to Nevada in the winter, and perhaps Atlantic City in the summer. That's the theory.

I live in the Midwest, and *my* preference is still Nevada. I like Reno in the summer, and Las Vegas in the winter. In July/August, Reno is usually in the 80's, while Las Vegas might be 110°! Too hot! In the winter months, Las Vegas hovers in the 60's and 70's. Reno can get downright chilly!

But climate isn't the only basis for my decision. If that was the case, point me towards Palm Springs!

I like Nevada because there are more casinos, more options, and more liberal blackjack rules. Plus, I like the sports books in Nevada, especially during the football season (Atlantic City does not have legalized sports-betting).

For now, Atlantic City is too crowded. Still not enough casinos! I don't want to compete with hundreds of other players who want the same table I do!

The game rules for blackjack are indeed more attractive in Nevada. There are no single-deck games in Atlantic City, mostly eight decks with two or three casinos now offering a six-deck shoe. Big Deal! If you play regularly in Atlantic City, I can only hope you're a craps-shooter!

In addition, pit bosses in Atlantic City seem overly concerned about counters. Certainly more so than in Nevada. Although recent court rulings have prevented casinos in Atlantic City from actually barring a player, pit bosses can and will instruct a dealer to "shuffle-up" frequently if they suspect a counter at their tables.

When I played there recently, in preparation for this book, I was shuffled-up on three times. When I sat out a few hands, a pit boss told me to either play or give up my chair. In Nevada, I like to watch a few hands during my play if the deck is 10-poor, or simply wait for a fresh shuffle. Obviously, I can't do this in Atlantic City when all the tables are full.

I suppose I can't blame them. They have plenty of people who want to play; who couldn't care less if the deck is 10-poor or 10-rich, and don't even know the difference!

Incidentally, this is a good time to mention another important factor to consider when choosing a casino. How well are you treated?

I only play in a casino where I know they appreciate my business, big or small, good or bad. If I'm treated rudely, that's it. If the service people are not pleasant, polite, and friendly, forget it.

Counter's Haven

Since Atlantic City cannot legally bar a player from blackjack, it does make it somewhat of a "haven" for counters.

When the court ruled in September 1982, Atlantic City casinos immediately put an eight-deck shoe into effect. They watched suspected counters with a special surveillance team. If the counter's bets were widely spread, the dealer would be told to shuffle-up. If the situation was considered serious, the pit boss would further instruct the dealer to cut 50% of the shoe. And that, my friend, is a damn good countermeasure! The counter has lost virtually all of his "skill."

Although the casinos have mellowed somewhat since then, they still are on the lookout for counters. The most blatant sign is the bet spread. And it's an important rule for you to remember. *Never vary your bets by more than 5 to 1*. For example, if you're playing a $5 minimum bet when the cards are average, don't press up more than five times that bet ($25) when the cards have turned in your favor. Unless you wish to alert the pit boss!

If you minimize the bet spread, the casino will generally let you play without any countermeasures, even if they know you're counting. So don't provoke it!

To my way of thinking, this whole discussion is academic.

Even without the countermeasures, a skilled counter has little chance of winning consistently. Too many decks! And for my Imperial Count, there are too many hands!

As you recall from an earlier chapter, multiple-decks tend to "normalize" the deck construction, and reduce the percentage of fluctuation.

Atlantic City casinos have little to worry about.

Hopefully, the increased competition among the casinos will bring about a one or two-deck game. And with more and more casinos, the crowds will thin out considerably. And sure, I realize that if you live in the East, Atlantic City is too convenient to pass up. But, until the casinos clear, and the rules improve, I strongly suggest you only play during weekdays, not weekends! But above all, play in Atlantic City with the utmost caution!

Incidentally, if you play craps . . . not blackjack, obviously it makes no difference whether you play in "Jersey" or Nevada. In fact, a number of Atlantic City casinos are offering double-odds! What more could you ask for?

Triple-odds?

That's right! I understand some Atlantic City casinos are now experimenting with triple-odds. Such a deal!

Casino Rules for Blackjack and Craps

Throughout this book, I've stressed the importance of playing where the rules are the most favorable to the player.

At the very least, the following chart will show you that the rules do indeed vary. But they also change. Obviously, the casino has the right to change their rules any time they want to.

Be sure to check with the casino at the time you play, to get a timely account of the rules.

Can I surrender? Can I double down on any two cards? Do you have double-odds? A professional player always asks these questions. You should also. It's an important part of your overall game-plan.

The information in the chart has been provided by the casino, based on our written survey. Rather than make a cursory review of the rules, we wanted the casinos to report *to us,* on our carefully prepared form.

Many didn't respond. You must not assume that the rules must be "poor" just because the casino's name doesn't appear on the list. As I said, several casinos simply wouldn't cooperate.

As you review the chart, look for "yes" as the favorable player condition. And look for one or two-deck games with small table minimums.

Above all, remember that the rules are not etched in stone. They are all subject to change.

THE REAL EXPERTS

Ever wonder who the real experts are at casino games?

The Library of Congress reports that over 500 books have been published on casino gambling. Are the authors all experts? What about the countless players who live in Nevada, and hit the tables day-in and day-out? Are *they* experts?

It's a trick question.

The true experts are the experienced pit bosses, and casino managers who have been in the gambling business a long, long time. Some over 40 years!

There's a casino manager at the Desert Inn, Russ Scott, who probably has forgotten more about gambling than the average player will ever learn in a lifetime! He can watch two dealers paying off 14 players and catch a $5 error. He knows every corner of the gambling industry, every gimmick, every rule, and all the percentages. Managers like Scott are the *real* experts. Make no mistake.

LAS VEGAS

NUMBER OF TABLES – TYPICAL WEEKEND EVENING

RULES SUBJECT TO CHANGE WITHOUT NOTICE

Note: The number-of-tables columns below are grouped by deck count; within each deck group the figures are listed by table minimum (\$2, \$5, \$25, \$100). "8 Decks" gives the total number of eight-deck tables. The final column is the craps "Double Odds" rule.

Casino	Double After Split	Surrender	Double on Any 2 Cards	Stand on All 17's	Player Cards Up	1 Deck	2 Decks	4 Decks	5 Decks	6 Decks	8 Decks	Double Odds
Circus Circus	No	No	No	No	No	29, , , 1	26, 4				5	No
Desert Inn	No	Yes	Yes	Yes	No				12, 14, 4, 2	2	6	No
Dunes	Yes	Yes	Yes	Yes	Yes	9			14, 24, 7, 3	3	9	Yes
Flamingo Hilton	No	Yes	No	No	No	24, 30, 4					7	No
4 Queens	No	No	No	No	No	16², 6¹, 9			13, 18, 2	1	6	Yes
Holiday	No	No	No	No	No	2			7³, 4, 1		5	Yes
Horseshoe	No	No	No	No	No	32, 2					9	Yes
Imperial Palace	No	Yes²	Yes	Yes	No	4, 6, 2			19		4	No
Landmark	No	No	Yes	No	No	7²				2	2	Yes
Marina	No	Yes	No	Yes	No	6			18, 2, 2		2	No
Maxim	No	No	No	No	Yes	7, 8, 11, 1			1		3	Yes
MGM Grand	Yes	No	No	No	No			10, 50, 29, 6			10	No
Mint	No	No	No	No	No	4, 3	18				6	Yes
Riviera	No	Yes	No	No	No	2, 2, 3, 2			10, 15, 3, 2	2	6	No
Sands	No	Yes	Yes	Yes	No	4	12		6		5	Yes
Tropicana	No	No	No	No	No		15, 10, 2, 2				9	Yes
Union Plaza	No	Yes¹	No	Yes	No	20, 6, 2		10			5	Yes
Vegas World	Yes	Yes	No	Yes	No	2	4, 4, 2, 2				2	Yes²

NUMBER OF TABLES – TYPICAL WEEKEND EVENING

RULES SUBJECT TO CHANGE WITHOUT NOTICE

	Double After Split	Double on Any 2 Cards	Surrender	Stand on All 17's	Player Cards Up	1 DECK $2	1 DECK $5	1 DECK $25	1 DECK $100	2 DECKS $2	2 DECKS $5	2 DECKS $25	2 DECKS $100	4 DECKS	5 DECKS $2	5 DECKS $5	5 DECKS $25	5 DECKS $100	6 DECKS $2	6 DECKS $5	6 DECKS $25	6 DECKS $100	8 DECKS $2	8 DECKS $5	8 DECKS $25	8 DECKS $100	CRAPS Tables	CRAPS Double	CRAPS Odds
ATLANTIC CITY																													
Bally's Park Place	Yes	Yes	No	Yes	Yes														35*	35	3	3					22	Yes	Yes
Caesars	Yes	Yes	No	Yes	Yes											50*	4										24	Yes	Yes
Claridge	Yes	Yes	No	Yes	Yes			2								30	8				2						12	Yes	Yes*
Resorts	Yes	Yes	No	Yes	Yes			4								30	6				2						20	Yes	Yes
Sands	No	Yes	No	Yes	Yes			1									4			16	39						16	Yes	Yes
Tropicana	Yes	Yes	No	Yes	Yes										12*	44*	18	6			6						18	Yes	Yes
NORTHERN NEVADA																													
Caesars Tahoe	Yes	Yes	No	Yes¹	18	9	2									6	6				2	1					6	No	No
Comstock	No	Yes	No	No	13	2											2				1						1	Yes	Yes
Eldorado	No	No	No	No	22	4																					2	Yes	Yes
High Sierra*	Yes*	Yes*	No	Yes*	14²	32	3									8				2							5	No	No
Holiday	No	No	No	No	7																1						1	Yes	Yes
Peppermill	No	Yes*	No	Yes*	11	4	1																				2	Yes	Yes

NO LIABILITY WILL BE ASSUMED FOR ERRORS OR OMISSIONS.

1 RESTRICTED TO TABLES WITH SHOE ONLY.
2 SOME TABLES ARE $1 MINIMUM.
3 SOME TABLES ARE $3 MINIMUM.
4 SOME TABLES ARE $10 MINIMUM.
5 TRIPLE ODDS.
6 FORMERLY SAHARA TAHOE.
7 FIVE-TIMES ODDS.

Casino's Win!

The casino industry is solid. No one builds $100 million hotels in a breakeven business.

I've told you about the staggering "win" revenue of casinos. Now, look at a 1982 income statement for all Atlantic City hotel/casinos combined. Notice the incredible spread between the casino revenue and all other income.

The total casino revenue *per day* for all nine casinos is over $4 million! It bears repeating. Each day, the casinos in Atlantic City win over $4 million! Perhaps the smart gambler doesn't play, he buys stock!

A similar chart for Las Vegas hotel/casinos (fiscal year ended June 30, 1982) is expressed in percentages. Notice that "Downtown" casinos reported that "gaming" represented nearly 70% of the total revenue. Take away the casinos and what do you have? Not much.

Perhaps our most interesting chart gives the "Percent of Revenue" from each game, for both "Strip" and "Downtown" hotel/casinos. Note that blackjack accounts for more than 25% of the total revenue on the strip. Slot machines account for more than 50% downtown!

Don't be misled. The ratio of the game revenue has no direct bearing on the house percentages. Blackjack leads craps for example, because there are so many more tables. Obviously, blackjack is much more popular than craps.

STATEMENT OF INCOME ALL CASINO HOTELS ATLANTIC CITY—1982

COURTESY: THE ATLANTIC CITY CASINO HOTEL ASSOCIATION.

	TOTAL INDUSTRY
REVENUES	
Casino	$1,484,750,464
Rooms	108,956,184
Food	155,970,917
Beverages	93,966,648
Other Operated Departments	31,176,220
Rentals and Other Income	8,086,500
Cover Charges and Minimums	22,467,413
Total Revenues	1,905,374,346
Less: Complimentary Services	189,333,476
Revenues, net of comp. serv.	1,716,040,870
COSTS AND EXPENSES	
Casino	651,855,565
Rooms	53,795,073
Food and Beverage	204,382,445
Other Operated Departments	36,114,529
Executive Office	37,755,127
Accounting and Auditing	25,377,635
Security	43,880,189
Other Administrative and General	59,893,925
Marketing	51,182,792
Guest Entertainment	43,570,525
Property Operation & Maintenance	45,436,240
Energy Costs	31,476,894
Rent, Property Taxes & Insurance	60,146,463
Interest Expense	111,521,723
Depreciation & Amortization	97,241,586
Total Costs and Expenses	1,553,630,710
OPERATING INCOME	162,410,160
Non-Operating Income (expenses), net	(44,377,239)
Gain or (loss) on disposal of property	4,958,306
INCOME BEFORE INCOME TAXES	122,991,227
PROVISIONS FOR INCOME TAXES	
Current	72,577,754
Deferred	76,519
Total Provisions for Income Taxes	72,654,273
INCOME BEFORE EXTRAORDINARY ITEMS	50,336,954
Extraordinary Items	6,561,000
NET INCOME	$ 56,897,954

CONDENSED INCOME STATEMENT—NEVADA
For the Year Ended June 30, 1982

	LAS VEGAS STRIP	DOWNTOWN LAS VEGAS	RENO/SPARKS AREA	SOUTH LAKE TAHOE	ELKO COUNTY	BALANCE OF STATE	STATEWIDE TOTAL
Number of locations	36	25	30	7	8	31	137
REVENUES							
Casino department	59.3%	69.7%	61.0%	59.7%	60.0%	63.4%	61.2%
Rooms department	14.8%	8.1%	10.2%	9.9%	5.5%	5.4%	11.8%
Food department	11.2%	10.3%	14.4%	14.6%	14.5%	15.3%	12.3%
Beverage department	8.2%	6.2%	9.4%	10.3%	8.8%	7.8%	8.3%
Other revenue	6.5%	5.7%	5.0%	5.5%	11.2%	8.1%	6.4%
Total revenues	100%	100%	100%	100%	100%	100%	100%
Cost of sales	6.8%	8.3%	10.1%	8.8%	13.4%	15.1%	8.5%
Gross margin	93.2%	91.7%	89.9%	91.2%	86.6%	84.9%	91.5%
Direct expense	45.5%	46.2%	42.2%	39.3%	40.8%	41.4%	44.0%
Departmental income	47.7%	45.5%	47.7%	51.9%	45.8%	43.8%	47.5%
Total general and admini- strative expenses	38.1%	36.7%	44.7%	51.2%	29.0%	36.8%	40.0%
Net operating income ...	9.6%	8.8%	3.0%	0.7%	16.8%	7.0%	7.5%

COURTESY: THE LAS VEGAS CONVENTION AND VISITORS AUTHORITY. SOURCE LISTED: NEVADA GAMING ABSTRACT—NEVADA GAMING CONTROL BOARD.

PERCENT OF REVENUE—LAS VEGAS
For the Year Ended June 30, 1982

	LAS VEGAS STRIP			DOWNTOWN LAS VEGAS		
	NUMBER OF LOCATIONS	NUMBER OF UNITS	PERCENT OF TOTAL GAMING REVENUE	NUMBER OF LOCATIONS	NUMBER OF UNITS	PERCENT OF TOTAL GAMING REVENUE
GAMES						
Twenty-one	38	927	25.5%	20	416	18.1%
Craps	35	149	16.5%	18	66	12.6%
Roulette	32	83	3.7%	19	34	1.7%
Other Games	25	89	14.5%	17	29	1.4%
Totals		1,248	60.2%		545	33.8%
DEVICES						
5¢ slot machine	40	6,451	4.6%	25	5,088	11.8%
10¢ slot machine	31	462	0.5%	24	361	1.0%
25¢ slot machine	41	7,114	10.7%	25	3,777	18.7%
50¢ slot machine	22	216	0.5%	13	128	0.9%
$1 slot machine	40	5,130	16.6%	25	2,164	21.2%
Other devices	27	739	1.3%	11	467	1.0%
Totals		20,112	34.2%		11,985	54.6%
OTHER GAMING						
Keno	28	30	3.0%	16	17	6.6%
Poker	21	163	1.8%	15	89	3.1%
Miscellaneous	11	22	0.8%	7	34	1.9%
Totals		215	5.6%		140	11.6%

COURTESY: THE LAS VEGAS CONVENTION AND VISITORS AUTHORITY. SOURCE LISTED: NEVADA GAMING ABSTRACT—NEVADA GAMING CONTROL BOARD.

Your Arsenal

Here's the point. It ain't easy! Put the pea-shooters away and listen up for a moment.

You now should know my way to beat the casino. Skill, smart betting, and strict discipline. You must be "conditioned" to win!

There are only three other ways to win that I know of: (1) you're lucky, (2) you cheat, or (3) you have ESP. Let's study each possibility.

First of all, "luck" is a four-letter word. No loyalties. "Lady Luck" has lots of boyfriends. No one is consistently lucky!

Cheating? You've got to be kidding! Never, even remotely consider it! Around Vegas, the desert gets mighty cold at 3 a.m. When I go jogging, I like to do it around the hotel!

Stories abound about cheating in casinos. I decided at the outset that cheat-stories were not fit for this book. I constantly hear about players trying to cheat a casino. Funny how you always hear about it, *after they're arrested*! Occasionally, you'll hear about a casino that allegedly cheated a player. Personally I doubt the validity of these stories, but to be safe, I make it a point to play only at major hotels where I couldn't possibly hurt the place with a few thousand win. By today's standards, and the priceless value of a gaming license, I wouldn't consider casino-cheating as a "priority" concern.

ESP? I know, there's always some nut who claims he can tell you what card's coming up, or what the dice will do. He's probably the same guy who tells you on Monday which football plays you should have made Sunday! If and when somebody walks into a casino and second guesses every card, it'll make headlines in every paper in the country. I'm waiting.

DO'S AND DON'TS

1. First and foremost, YOU MUST HAVE A STRONG DESIRE TO WIN.

2. DON'T GET GREEDY AT THE TABLES! A win *is a win*. Period!

3. BET SAFELY, especially at the beginning of each session.

4. SET ASIDE SOME WINNINGS, to insure that you leave the table ahead!

5. PLAY ONLY WHEN YOU'RE RELAXED, ALERT, AND READY. Never when you're tired.

6. PLAY AT YOUR OWN PACE. Don't play on credit, looking for a comp.

7. FOLLOW YOUR INSTINCTS. If you think you're about to lose. Quit!

8. LEARN THE GAMES THOROUGHLY. Don't wager a single dollar until you know exactly what you're doing.

9. MAKE THE RIGHT BETS. Know the proper bets to make, and bets never to consider.

10. PRESS UP WHEN YOU'RE WINNING. LAY BACK WHEN YOU'RE LOSING.

11. SET A FIRM LIMIT ON ANY LOSSES.

12. NEVER JUMP OUT OF A STREAK. Follow my "press" schedules and win it big!

13. SEEK OUT THE VERY BEST PLAYING CONDITIONS. Look for casinos that give you the best chance to win.

14. At blackjack, MEMORIZE BASIC STRATEGY AND PLAY THE IMPERIAL COUNT.

15. Find the discipline to ONLY PLAY HEAD-ON, preferably at a one or two-deck game.

16. At craps, PLAY WITH DOUBLE-ODDS. And make only pass-line, come-bets, and odds-bets.

17. Most important of all, LEARN TO RECOGNIZE AN OPPORTUNITY. Then strike! When the opportunity has vanished, quit.

Remember what I told you earlier. Of all the strategies, common sense and keen discipline are still the best strategies of all!

If you remember anything, remember that there are no guarantees. If it just isn't your night, quit! There's always tomorrow.

Hopefully, you'll review each and every page of this book before you play. Don't just skim . . . oops, I promised many of my friends in Vegas that I wouldn't use that word. Don't just *skip* through the book. Read it again, every word. Refer to it often.

I wish you the best of success!